DISCARD

THE RED-HOT RATTOONS

THE RED-HOT RATTOONS

by **ELIZABETH WINTHROP**

with drawings by
BETSY LEWIN

Henry Holt and Company · New York

Acknowledgments

I am grateful to Kim La Rue and Adriene Thorne
for their invaluable input on dance; to Peter,
Margaret, Betsy, and Marion for their close readings
of this story in its different incarnations; and
to "red-hot" Dylan once again.

Henry Holt and Company, LLC
Publishers since 1866
115 West 18th Street
New York, New York 10011
www.henryholt.com

Library of Congress Cataloging-in-Publication Data
Winthrop, Elizabeth.
The Red-Hot Rattoons / by Elizabeth Winthrop.
p.   cm.
Summary: After the death of their parents, five young rats decide to leave the barnyard
to make a name for themselves in the big city, facing unscrupulous rivals and
dangerous humans along the way.
[1. Rats—Fiction.   2. Brothers and sisters—Fiction.
3. City and town life—Fiction.]   1. Title.
PZ7.W768Re2003   [Fic]—dc21   2002038880

ISBN 0-8050-7229-2
First Edition—2003
Printed in the United States of America on acid-free paper.∞
1   3   5   7   9   10   8   6   4   2

FOR MY MOTHER
WHO SHARES WITH ELLA A LOVE OF JAZZ
AND THE COURAGE TO VENTURE
INTO THE UNKNOWN

CONTENTS

THE RED-HOT RATTOONS

1

THE CALL OF THE DANCE

Once in a barnyard there lived five gray rats along with the usual assortment of cows, horses, geese, ducks, sheep, turkeys, a mule, some pigs, and a couple of goats.

The rats' names were Benny, Fletcher, Ella, Woody, and Monk. As you might have already guessed, they were the children of accomplished musicians. Their father, a trumpet player named Art Hornblower, had been born on the seamy side of New Orleans, where the music flowed in the streets as easy as the river in its banks. He had proposed to their mother, a singer named Sally Scat Rat, the first time she opened her mouth to sing "A Fine Rat Romance" in a dance palace called Funky Joey's. They traveled north on the riverboats to Chicago and then east on the Midnight Express. They sang at Snout's Ballroom, the Boom Boom Room, and all the other hip joints in New York and made quite a name for themselves. But after a while they tired of the noise and bustle of the city. Sally wanted children, and Art agreed to move north to farm country, where they

3

could raise a family in peace. They found a cozy nest in the cellar of a large barn. Whenever the horse or the mule stamped a hoof up above, a lovely rainfall of grain sifted down through the cracks in the floor.

Two nights a week, Art and Sally had a regular gig at the Blue Goat, a local jazz and blues club. On the nights they were booked to sing, patrons came from all around the county and lined the lane, waiting for the first-come, first-served seats.

One night, to everybody's surprise, Switchtail, an old friend from the city, showed up at the Goat. There was a great deal of weeping and backslapping. The five children were trotted out and introduced to their uncle Switch, who settled himself at Art and Sally's reserved table in the front row so he could record the pair for his new label, Ratty Music Records. Under this same table, with Switchtail's foot tapping out the rhythm next to their heads, the five rat kids fell asleep to the sweet sound of their mother's voice playing tag with the notes from their father's horn.

Benny and his siblings knew everybody at the Goat, and everybody knew them. Fletcher drew pictures with his paw in the sawdust under the table. Monk, the youngest, roamed the place, looking for treats. The regulars knew to slip him tidbits only when Sally was busy singing. The bartender answered the million questions Ella asked him about everything from how the spout on the mash barrel worked to how he tied that fancy knot with his apron strings. Woody sat on Uncle Switch's lap and learned to adjust the levels on the boom box in order to catch that low sultry note of their mother's voice or the clear high C from their father's horn.

It was a routine they liked. Most of the time they lived their regular barnyard existence, and then two exciting nights a week, they made their way with Ma and Pa to the Blue Goat, where the lights were dim, the air was smoky, and music hugged the walls. The days passed like that, and nobody thought they would ever change. But life has a way of handing out surprises.

Late one night, the rat children woke to the noise of screaming, the rumble of a truck engine, and the tramp of human feet. Paws dragged them from under the table and passed them above the melee to the door, where they were thrown out into the night. The last thing they heard was Switchtail's voice above the noise. "Run for your lives," he shouted. "Home to the barnyard. Don't look back."

Benny picked up Monk and led the rest away from the Goat across the pasture through the darkness. When they reached the barnyard gate, the five of them slithered under the rough wood and came to rest in a pile of hay in the mule's stall.

The mule opened one eye and surveyed the clutch of shivering gray bodies. "You're back early tonight. Where's your folks?" he asked.

"We don't know," cried Ella. "Everybody screamed at us to run and we ran."

"From the Blue Goat?"

"That's right."

"Who're you talking to?" asked the horse, poking his head over the divider between their stalls.

"The rat kids. Sounds like there's been trouble over at the Blue Goat. Sounds like the farmer made good on his promise."

"What promise?" asked Benny, drawing himself out of the pile of his siblings. Since he was the oldest, he figured he'd better act it.

"Now, now," said the horse, who had a soft spot for small creatures. "We won't know for sure till the morning. But you kids better prepare yourself for bad news. Sounds like the exterminators."

"The what?" shrieked Fletcher, the most excitable.

"I know what they are," said Benny in a low voice. "The farmer sends them out to poison rats."

"That's right," said the mule. "And lately the house cat's been hearing him talk about that old shack down by the river being infested with rats."

"The Blue Goat is not a shack," said Woody, who was very precise. "It's a nightclub. Best one in ten counties. And our parents are the best jazz duo in twenty."

"It may be a nightclub to you, young fella," said a goat who had ambled over to join the conversation. "But to that farmer, it's a falling-down shack and a harbor for vermin."

"What's vermin?" asked Ella.

"We're vermin," said Benny. "According to humans and cats. And exterminators, I guess."

A couple of foxes went over to the Blue Goat the next day and reported that the shack had been knocked down and plowed under and there was no sign of a rat anywhere near.

"They escaped," Fletcher said loudly. "They'll come back."

Four pairs of eyes looked at him and slid away.

The barnyard did their best to adopt the rat family. The mule and the horse stamped their hooves often so that the grain sifted down on a regular schedule. One of the cows let it be known that she was happy to have them drop by her stall anytime. A couple of ducks taught them how to swim as a distraction.

But mostly the rat kids kept to themselves, waiting for something to happen. None of them was sure what that might be.

As the weeks went by, Benny noticed that the bellies of his three brothers and his one sister dragged along the ground. They slept on their backs in the summer. A really hot rat sleeps on his back so he can sweat through the soles of his feet. But Benny noticed that his brothers and sister were sleeping on their backs as the days grew colder. Their bellies had grown too large to be comfortable in any other position.

"We're getting too fat," he announced one day after lunch, which had almost immediately followed breakfast.

"Too fat for what?" asked Ella, who asked more questions than the other four put together.

"Too fat to prowl the barnyard or run in the fields. Ma and Pa would have expected more of us," Benny said.

"Like what?" asked Woody.

"Something to do," said Benny. "Somebody to be. They were famous."

"I miss Ma and Pa," said Fletcher.

"We all miss them," said Benny. "And we've got to do something that would make them proud."

"What?" asked Ella.

For a long time that afternoon, they sat in a circle and tried to think what they could possibly do to make their parents proud. But nothing came to them, which made them feel even gloomier than before.

They ate dinner early, went to bed as soon as the sun had set, and slept through most of the next day.

2

THE RETURN OF SWITCHTAIL

A familiar voice woke them. "Now, this is a fine collection of lazypaws," it announced from the top of a grain bin.

"Who's that?" cried Monk, struggling up from sleep.

"Uncle Switch," Ella cried. "Wake up, everybody, it's Uncle Switch."

The rest of them scrabbled to a sitting position. Switchtail slid down the edge of the bin and waded into the hay to throw his limbs around them. "I've been thinking about this here moment for so long," Switch said. "You kids okay?"

Settled against the soft graying fur of his belly, they shrugged, one after another.

"Got a little heft on you, I see," he said.

"Too much," Benny reported. "We've been eating fine. Not doing much else."

"Ma and Pa?" Monk squeaked.

Switch sighed. "Best rats that ever were."

Fletcher asked the question on all their minds. "Are they coming back, Uncle Switch?"

"No, Fletcher, my rat. They won't be coming back."

As soon as the awful words were out of his mouth, Switch's belly began to shake, and pretty soon they were all crying. It didn't seem possible that it would ever stop. As soon as one of them would sniff for the last time, another would go off in a wail. It wasn't a bad thing, though. Sometimes crying is absolutely one hundred percent necessary.

Silence descended. Every tear they had been holding inside had at last been shed.

"How did you get out?" Ella asked in a small voice.

"It was a miracle. I owe my life to a bunch of rats from the next county who carried me home with them and nursed me. They even saved my box and all my tapes. Couldn't hardly lift my head off the hay pile for months. Soon as I got my strength back, I came looking for you all."

"You still going to make those recordings you talked about?" Woody asked.

"Been thinking about it. But first I had to make sure you were settled. You kids got any ideas for your future?"

The five looked at one another.

"We were trying to figure that out just yesterday," Benny said.

"But we couldn't think of anything," said Fletcher.

"Well, I got an idea," said Switch. He pulled the boom box from the sack of belongings he'd stashed behind the grain bin.

He lined them up and told them to close their eyes. They heard the plink of piano keys, the kiss of the drum brush, and the low thump of the bass man working his strings. Then from somewhere on the other side of the moon came the sweet high notes of their father's trumpet, followed by their mother's voice singing, "A fine rat romance with no kisses. A fine romance, my rat mate, this is . . ."

They didn't open their eyes but stood swaying from side to side. The music flowed through them from oldest to youngest, and they began to move. Benny led the way. "One, two, three," he counted, and five right legs stepped together, ten shoulders lifted in time. "Four, five, six," and five left legs found the ground. Their bellies bounced this way and that, but the rats slid their way across the basement floor and sidled their way back again. It was as if someone had choreographed their every move, as if their arms and legs were connected by invisible wires. Monk brought up the rear, his head thrown back with great abandon. When the music stopped, the air felt emptier than it had before.

"Just as I thought," said Switchtail's voice.

They opened their eyes and looked around, dazed, as if they were waking from a dream.

"You are going to be dancers."

"You think so, Uncle Switch?" said Monk, who was trying out a little soft shoe on his own.

"We're good, aren't we?" said Fletcher.

"You're fine for beginners. But you got a lot of hard work ahead of you," said Switch.

"You can teach us?" asked Ella.

"If I can't, nobody can. Don't you know that your old uncle here is one of the best dancers in the neighborhood, never mind this county and all of Rat Hollow? The whole world, maybe." He gave his long whiskers a proud twirl.

"I thought you were a recording rat," said Woody.

"That's my new gig. You never did hear about my old gig, did you?"

They shook their heads.

"Originally my ancestors came from New York City, but I started out in the South just like your ma and pa," he explained. "In those days, if you were a rat with music in your soul, soon as you could, you headed north for the Hollow. It was the only place to be. I danced my way right up the coast, and by the time I arrived, I was one of the best lindy hoppers around. Me and my partner, Fannie Mae."

"What dances did you do?" Woody asked.

"All of them, kid. Top to bottom. The Mooch, the Slow Drag, the Big Apple, the Snake Hips, the Rat's Tail. Fannie Mae and me, we made that one up. Rats used to travel miles to Snout's Ballroom just to see Switch lift Fannie over his head. Yes, sirree, we tore up the floor at Snout's."

"What happened to her?" Ella asked.

"Ran off with a West Coast rat by name of Loosehips who said he could get her into the movies. Twenty years, I never let that girl's name pass my lips. Left Snout's, moved my act down to Ratland. Kept dancing. Got myself some new partners, and those ladies taught me the Stroll and the Slop and the Monkey."

"And you can teach us how to dance?" said Fletcher.

"Well, I can try. I've been wondering whether you five might have some talent in that direction, considering your musical heritage." He sat in silence, thinking, and after a while, a little gleam came into his eye. "Maybe one day you'll dance at the Boom Boom Room."

"What's that?" asked Benny.

"Your parents had a gig there when it was a jazz and blues place. But it fell on hard times, and the new owners turned it into a swanky dance palace with a stage show."

"Where is it?" Monk asked.

"Down in Rat Hollow, over in the musical part of town. Underneath the Crystal."

"What's Rat Hollow?" Ella asked. "And the Crystal?"

Switch's jaw dropped open. "You mean your ma and pa didn't tell you about the Hollow?"

The five heads shook back and forth, and Switch was glad to see their snouts moved in perfect unison. But he was having second thoughts.

"Maybe I need to reconsider this whole idea. Sally was determined to bring her babies up out here in the country. I don't want to go against her wishes. Maybe I shouldn't tell you about all this stuff. Maybe we better come up with some other plan for your future."

"No," cried the five. "We want to dance at the Boom Boom Room."

"The country is boring," said Fletcher.

"It's our musical heritage," Woody said.

The old rat waited for silence.

"You sure?"

"We're sure," they shouted, jumping up and down.

"Well," he said, "first we got some rearranging to do. You all are moving up to the loft. No more slacking around down here, waiting for the grain to fall into your mouths. You rats need to slim down if you're going to dance."

3

RAT HOLLOW

On the new regimen, Switchtail chivied the five out of their nest in the mornings and taught them the virtues of regular exercise. They sweated their way through push-ups, sit-ups, and tail curls. They squatted, they stretched, and they straddled. They pumped iron on a strange machine Woody invented out of bridles and a set of mattress springs. Their bellies waned. Their muscles swelled.

Once they'd trimmed down, Switch started them at the barre.

Monk complained, "Why do we have to learn these funny positions?"

"Ballet, my boy, is the foundation of all dance. Put that paw back on the barre. Now pliés. Deeper. Okay, eyes front. Again. Drop from your hips, Benny. Stop that slouching, Fletcher. Lift your chin, Ella. You don't want to go around with your chin buried in your chest. Be a proud rat and show it. Snout in the air, chin out."

Ella nodded. She blinked and two tears ran down her cheeks, but Switch pretended not to notice. These kids had to toughen up. Rat Hollow was no picnic.

Slowly the five learned to do their jetés, their battements, and their pas de bourrées with attitude. They strutted, they marched, they dug their toes and threw back their heads. And at night they fell into their nest, moaning in pain.

○　●　○　●　○

Switch produced from his sack a pile of old tap shoes.

Ella's feet were a little small for her shoes, but he stuffed the toes with shredded newspaper.

He started them off with the basic steps: toe taps, brushes, hops, slaps, cramp rolls, and pullbacks. Then he moved on to the Boogie Woogie, the Shorty George, and the Shuffle Off to Buffalo. Their eyes rolled in their heads at all the things they were trying to learn at once.

"Now, you give me one regular shim sham, a stomp, then three shuffles, ball-change. Keep those hips facing front, those eyes straight ahead. All right, ready. STOP." Switchtail put up his paw. "I am waiting for quiet feet, and I don't intend to wait long."

He glared at the smallest rat, who was lost in a little shuffle of his own at the back of the line. Monk couldn't get over the delicious clicking noise his feet now made, and he tickled the planking of the barn floor with his steel toes whenever he got the chance.

"Sorry," he whispered.

"You keep those feet locked up, Monk, till I say they can go or you're out on your tail," said Uncle Switch with a curl of his upper lip. "Second position. Five, six, seven, eight."

Off they went in a diagonal line from hay bin to water trough and back again, their tails lifted, their toes cocked high to stomp and then dropped low to brush the floor. And always above them they heard the rasp of Switchtail's voice. "Woody, flat feet make me crazy. Lift those heels. Ella, chin up. Good, now drop into a sugar walk. Twist those hips, move those shoulders. Benny, rubber limbs. Loose and easy."

He made them dance without music so they understood that they were the instruments, that their feet made the beat. "You are making shoe music," he called above the noise of their taps. "Listen to yourselves. Hook those feet up to those ears. Fletcher, you're off, way off. Quit rattling around and start again. Get into that rhythm or get out of the line. I want to hear the beat coming out of your feet."

Switch took them through their ballet positions again and again, but now he loosened their knees and let their limbs fly. He taught them how to isolate their shoulders and swivel their hips.

"Every move you make," he said, "you tell yourselves that's the very last time you're ever going to make that move. You give it everything you got. Or don't you bother me or the audience with yourselves. We got better things to do. You hear?"

They heard.

One day Switchtail sat them in a circle. "Now, I'm going to give you all a little talk about the city. It's different from the country, and you got to be prepared. Here in the barnyard, the animals and the humans run into each other now and again, but we don't need to see too much of the humans, and that's a good thing. But in New York, there are two cities, one right on top of the other. The top level is the human city. Down below is Rat Hollow. Of course, the Hollow is where you five'll be hanging out. You're never going to go aboveground to where the humans live. Never. That's the most important lesson you got to remember. You hear me?"

Switchtail's voice had a strange urgency to it they had not heard before. They nodded solemnly.

"Monk, I'm speaking to you specially. You got yourself what I call an adventuresome spirit. Now, you put that into your dancing."

"Yes, sir," Monk whispered.

"Some rats have special jobs up above in the human city, such as gathering food and goods for those of us in the Hollow. But the rats who try to go aboveground without any purpose or permission—" His voice ground to a halt, and he shook his head. "A few came back to tell the tale. Not many."

"But what about the Boom Boom Room?" Ella asked.

"What about it?"

"Is it in Rat Hollow?"

Switchtail clapped his paw to his forehead. "Lordy, I have some educating to do here. Everything you're going to need is in the Hollow. You're going to be living in a world surrounded by your own kind, a place the humans don't even know about. Of course, they seen evidence of us and they try to rid themselves of us with all sorts of nasty poisons. But they got no idea what a civilization we made right under their feet. No idea." He closed his eyes, remembering. "It's truly a wonder."

"What will we eat?" asked Woody. "If there's no barnyard, then there's no grain."

Switchtail's eyes gleamed. "Rat, once you been to the Hollow, you'll never settle for grain again. The whole place is your dining room. There's food beyond your wildest dreams."

"Where does it come from?" Benny asked.

"From up above. The humans drop it. Remember when you were sleeping down in the cellar and the grain would just fall into your mouths? Well, in the Hollow, the food rains down on you like manna from heaven."

"What kind of food?" Monk wanted to know.

"Human food. Things called nachos and potato chips and pizza. Now, pizza used to be my own personal favorite. It's a kind of pancake that they invented across the ocean in some foreign place." He closed his eyes for a minute, and his incisors slipped out over his lower lip as if in anticipation of this special delicacy. "It has cheese," he murmured. Then he shook himself. "No more talking about food."

"If the humans feed us, they can't be that bad," said Fletcher.

"They don't feed us on purpose," Switch snapped. "They're just too lazy to make their way to a garbage can, so they drop the food where they stand. And we get the benefit."

"When did Rat Hollow start?" asked Benny.

"In the last century. About the time the humans started using cement in their buildings. Nobody can make a burrow in that stuff. It's like trying to dig a hole in a rock. Then they invented something called the car, and the stables started shutting down one by one. Rats kept losing their homes. No place left for us to go. Then they built the Crystal. That was the final blow."

"What's the Crystal?" Ella asked.

"The humans' dance palace. Largest one in their world. They knocked down a whole row of great jazz clubs to build it. Ruined thousands of our burrows and wiped out a good number of our species in the process. My great-grandfather was lost there, according to family lore. So that's when the Founder rats decided to create the Hollow. They wanted to make sure we never mixed with humans again except when absolutely necessary for the livelihood of the species. Took some time to build, but we did it."

"The humans call their palace the Crystal?" asked Fletcher.

"No. The Crystal is our name for it. The human name for it never passes the lips of any rat. Too many of our ancestors' bones are buried under there."

"Do you know the human name?" Benny asked.

Switchtail stared at him for a long time. "And if I did, what difference would it make, Benny? You're never going to hear me say it." His voice held a mixture of such sadness and disappointment that Benny wished the stupid question had never come out of his mouth.

"So all the humans are bad," Woody said to fill the silence.

"Every single one of them is out to get us," Switchtail said. "Look what happened down at the Goat. Don't you ever forget that." He was silent for a moment. "There was one," he said after a while. "Never met him, but he's a kind of legend."

They drew closer.

"His name was Oliver String Bean Bailey, and the story goes, he was raised in an orphanage, one of those places humans put the babies with no parents."

"Like us," said Benny.

"Except we got Uncle Switch," said Fletcher.

"That's right, like you all. And maybe this Oliver had his own Uncle Switch because he made friends with a rat named Barney that lived under the radiator in his room. The human taught Barney tricks. How to do a snout stand and turn somersaults and hold himself up with just his tail."

"How can you do that?" Woody asked.

"Darn near impossible, but I talked to rats who swore they'd seen him do it. Anyway, Barney taught this man, well, he was just a boy then, how to speak our language. And the man never forgot it."

"Rats understand human language," Benny said. "Pa told me that. We're just born with that kind of higher intelligence."

"And your pa was right. But no human has ever bothered to learn our language. Until this one."

"Did you ever meet Oliver Bailey?" Monk asked.

"No. But I heard about him often enough. He managed some groups of performing rats and took them to shows aboveground. Rumor was he was trying to make humans see that we are a noble and dignified species and that we deserve our place in the world." Switchtail shrugged. "Sounds like a rat's tale to me, but you don't ever know, do you?"

4

JOBƒ

They continued to rehearse in the mornings. At five every evening, Switchtail taught a class called Rules for Daily Living in Rat Hollow.

Since Monk was the roamer, he was put in charge of navigation. Switch produced a series of maps of the Hollow.

"This is the side you use," Switch said.

"What's on the other side?" Monk asked.

"Aboveground. Nothing you need to know about. These maps are old, but they're all I got. The newer ones don't even mention the place." Switch taught him how to find north, east, south, and west and ordered him to memorize the stops on all the train lines. He made him a carrying tube for the maps that hung like a quiver from his shoulder.

Ella was appointed dance captain. She would be responsible for taking them through warm-ups and for scheduling their rehearsals. Switch began to give her lessons in the basics of choreography.

Woody was to carry the boom box and the tapes in his backpack and make sure they were well maintained.

"What's Benny going to do?" Ella asked.

"Benny is the oldest, so he's in charge," said Switchtail. "Whenever there's a decision that's got to be made, you all better listen to him." He glared at the four younger ones. "That's the way your ma and pa would've laid it down." The grumbling subsided.

"What about me?" Fletcher asked.

"I got you a special job, since you're the artistic one in the family," said Switch. He dragged out a trunk that he had stored in the corner of the loft some days before. "You're the costume captain."

"What's a costume?" asked Ella.

"I'll show you," said Switchtail. He dove into the trunk and came up with what looked like a bunch of rags. "The Hollow is a sophisticated place. Every rat wears clothes like the humans. Now, come on over here, Fletcher, and help me out."

By the time they were through, Fletcher and Switchtail had sorted the clothes into five piles. Each of them had only two outfits since, as Switch explained, they needed to travel light. Fletcher would carry the wardrobe suitcase.

"What's this?" Benny asked, holding out a black circle.

"That's a top hat," said Switch as he snapped it and settled it on Benny's head. "Perfect fit."

It took them a while to get used to the idea of clothes. Switch taught Fletcher how to use a needle and thread, and after some alterations, the five of them, in tuxedos and top hats, stood in line for inspection.

"Not bad," Switch said, walking up and down. "Not bad at all." He straightened Monk's collar, rubbed a spot off Ella's shoe, and adjusted Woody's hat. "Fletcher, I do believe you got some talent for this."

Fletcher beamed.

"Now, soon as you can, go see Frankie at the Ratpaws," Switchtail said. "He's got the best dance shoe store in the Hollow, and he knows everything about tap shoes. Frankie'll fix you up with rubber pads so you don't slip no matter what turf you dance on. Monk, I'll give you the address later so you can locate it on the map."

○　●　○　●　○

"Do you think we'll make it?" Benny asked one day after a lunch break.

They waited for Switchtail's answer.

"Can't say for sure," Switch said. "You got rhythm, you got some style, now you need to get yourselves some dancing experience. You know what they first called jazz, this music you're dancing to?"

They shook their heads.

"Ratty music. This was our music before it ever belonged to anybody else." He pulled himself to his feet and dusted the last bits of grain off his belly. "I got a name for your group. From now on, you call yourselves the Rattoons."

"Why?" Ella asked.

"Because a rattoon is the shoot that sprouts out of the root of the sugarcane plant once it's been cut down. You five came from Art and Sally's roots. You got a tradition to carry on. You got their beat in your blood and their notes in your bones."

"Our parents were cut down," Benny said.

"In their prime," Switchtail replied.

There was a moment of silence.

"The Rattoons," Monk said, rolling the sound around on his tongue.

"It sounds good," said Fletcher.

"Of course it does," Switchtail said. "Now, back to work."

○   ●   ○   ●   ○

In the weeks that followed they almost gave up. Their muscles had hardened and their toes had toughened, but now came the most difficult part of all. They had to learn the routines that Switchtail had worked out for them. He was relentless.

"No, Woody!" he would thunder, marching onto the floor. "I'll show you one more time. Start with your right foot. Walk, walk, ball-change, step. Make it look tough. You're strutting. Then spin to the front." He spun. "Right, left, change step. Stomp, stomp, shuffle."

They all stared as if they could suck his every move right into their bones just by watching him. He made it look easy, but it wasn't. They had grown used to their muscles aching, but now it was their heads that hurt from trying to remember where each paw was supposed to be.

They fell into bed in the loft too tired to eat, and all night long their bodies twitched to the bark of Switchtail's voice. They breathed to a count of eight, slept to a count of eight, rose to a count of eight, and chewed their breakfast to a count of eight.

And then one day, it happened. They didn't need to think anymore. Their muscles were hooked to the music. The dance danced them. At the end of a long rehearsal, Ella looked over to see that Switchtail was crying.

"Did we do it wrong again?" she asked.

"No, my girl. You did it right, so right." He slunk out the door, brushing tears from his cheeks.

"Is he okay?" Monk asked.

"I think he's remembering the old days at Snout's," Benny said.

"With Fannie Mae," Woody said.

"I wish he would come with us to the Hollow," Fletcher said.

"He told me his bones have grown too stiff for cement," Benny said. "Only reason he'll come is to see us dance at the Boom Boom Room."

5

OFF TO THE HOLLOW

Before their departure, Switchtail gave each of them a word of private advice. He warned Monk again about wandering. "That nose you got for food can lead you down some dangerous paths," said Switch. "It's your job to follow the maps. The rest of them depend on you for that."

He gave Fletcher last-minute tips on costume repair and wrote out the address for the Ratpaws. "Moment you get to the Hollow, you get everybody in their clothes. Don't want my Rattoons looking like a bunch of country rats."

He spent an entire afternoon showing Woody how to take apart the boom box and put it back together. Then he handed over the duplicate tapes he'd made for their routines.

"Don't you need to keep the box?" Woody asked. "What will you use for your recordings?"

"Never mind about that. I'll rustle up more equipment," Switchtail said. "You are talking to a rat with connections."

With Ella, he went over the combinations for their routines. "Don't let your brothers slack off, girl. Make sure you all rehearse every day. And then you start making up some of your own steps and moves. You got talent in that direction." Ella grinned.

The last was Benny.

"You got your paws full with this here pack of rats, my boy," said Switchtail when he took Benny to one side the morning of their departure. "Now you keep your eyes open and your mouths shut. Make all the noise you want to make with your feet. Your dancing, that's the only way to bring attention to yourselves."

"Right, Uncle Switch," Benny said.

Switchtail opened his arms and gave each one of them a bone-crushing hug.

Then Benny stood apart and squared his shoulders. In a voice that was stronger than the trembles in his belly, he said, "All right, Rattoons, we're on our way. Double time down the hill if we're going to make that train."

They set off at a trot. Monk looked back once and waved at Switchtail, who was standing like a statue in the barnyard door. The next time Monk looked, the old rat had disappeared from sight.

o   •   o   •   o

Uncle Switch had shown them where to hide themselves in the housing above the wheels while the train was sitting in the station.

The train ride was smooth enough. Sitting side by side,

Fletcher and Woody used the boom box as a backrest. The slap and bump of the wheels against the rails set their toes to tapping, and before long, they had figured out a way to practice their routines moving only their feet.

Monk explored, jumping from one perch to another until Benny ordered him to stay in one place because he was making them all dizzy.

"Don't be grumpy, Benny," Ella called from up above, where she was curled into a tight little corner, her tail tucked neatly around her. "We're going to the big city. Soon we're going to open at the Boom Boom Room and rats will come from all over Rat Hollow to watch us dance. We'll be famous."

Benny nodded, but he had his misgivings. He'd sat through enough late-night sessions with Switchtail to know that the days ahead were not going to be easy. At the end of those evenings, he'd tumbled into bed, his head stuffed with warnings. "Don't do this. Make sure to do that. Whatever happens, don't do the other. . . ." How was he going to keep it all straight?

The train was slowing. Ella hung upside down to peer at the passing scenery.

"No more trees," she announced. "Just buildings, one after another, marching along."

They entered a tunnel and traveled in total darkness for quite some time.

"Get ready," Benny said. "Stay right behind me.

Switchtail gave me directions for getting down to Rat Hollow. We don't want any humans to see us."

With a nasty squeal of metal scraping metal, the train lurched to a stop. Up above, they could hear the doors sliding open and the rush of footsteps on the platform.

One by one they dropped to the tracks and made their way to the front end of the train, where Benny led them deep into the black darkness of the tunnel. He'd memorized the directions. Turn left after the fourth pillar to the north and then pass the large door covered with wildly colored drawings and letters.

"What's that?" Benny had asked Switchtail.

"Art. They call it graffiti. The door itself actually leads to some kind of storeroom for the humans. But you don't need to concern yourself with that. You keep going exactly ten rat steps. There'll be another smaller, rat-sized door on your left. It's locked, but if you slip the tip of your tail into the keyhole, it will open."

"What about cats?" Benny had asked. "Do their tails fit?"

"Only hairless tails work," Switchtail had told him. "There are tail openers in specific places all over the city for rats to move safely back and forth. But once you make your way down to Rat Hollow, you are not to go aboveground. For *any* reason."

Benny had nodded wearily. Switchtail must have repeated this warning ten times a day.

He slipped his tail into the hole, and the door swung open. The five of them made their way down the metal steps toward the light and bustle of another train platform. But what a different and miraculous place this was.

A sleek silver train stood in the station with the doors open. Rats in bowler hats and smart three-piece suits marched along the platform. Many of them carried briefcases, and some were reading a newspaper called *The Rat Tales*. There were lady rats in polka-dot dresses and wide-brimmed hats, swinging pocketbooks off one shoulder and sometimes a briefcase from the opposite paw. These rats didn't ride in the housing next to the wheels. They marched right through the rat-sized doors and settled themselves comfortably on the seats or hung from the straps.

A conductor in a blue uniform spoke over the loudspeaker. "All aboard, watch the closing doors. Mind your tails and whiskers." Passengers scuttled to jump aboard, and the train rolled smoothly out of the station.

Best of all, there was a comforting and familiar smell that they had only really known when they were piled together under the table at the Blue Goat. This was a smell that meant they were with their own kind. It was not that they had disliked the odors of the barnyard, but this smell meant home and ancestry. It rooted them to their past.

For some time, the five stood transfixed on the platform

and breathed in the pure and comforting aroma of rat. A mother rat pushed past them with two young children. They both pointed at the Rattoons.

"Look, Ma. They don't have any clothes on."

"Quick," Fletcher said. "Get into your costumes."

6

SHADRACH

Once dressed, they made their way through the hurrying crowds toward the end of the platform.

"All of them rats," Fletcher said in awe as they scampered down a set of steps. "I never thought there were so many of us."

Benny knocked on a door decorated with a picture of a hat and cane.

"Who's there?" roared a voice from the other side.

"It's the Rattoons, Mr. Shadrach," Benny called out. "Mr. Switchtail sent us."

After a considerable silence, the door swung open. A rat with salt-and-pepper-colored fur towered over them. His belly was covered with bits of food despite the large soiled napkin tied around his neck. His top hat perched precariously above one ear, and when he looked down the row of the five rats standing on his doorstep, the hat toppled off his head and rolled away into the blackness behind him.

"Switch sent word about visitors," he muttered with a curl of his lip. "I didn't expect so many."

"We don't need to stay, Mr. Shadrach," Benny said in a voice twice the size of his courage. "We just wanted to introduce ourselves."

"Pleased to meet you," said Shadrach, and slammed the door.

The five looked at one another, but before they could speak, the door opened again. "Just a joke," he said, waving them inside. "Come on in. Can't have a pile of country rats littering my doorsill. Word would start to get around, give me a bad name."

It was a cozy place. Postage stamps decorated the walls, and a number of round silver disks had been stacked on top of one another to make a side table. Over in the corner a pile of pretty green-and-white paper had been chewed into what looked like a comfortable nest.

"Those are dollars," Woody whispered to Fletcher.

"What are dollars?"

"I found one under the stable floor one day and showed it to the horse. He said humans use them to steal things from each other. And the side table. That's made of quarters. More human money."

"Nice color green," said Fletcher as he bounced up and down on the bed. "Soft too. Maybe we can find some to make our nests."

Ella put her nose in the air and sniffed. There was a strong odor of something that reminded the young rats of their nights under the table at the Blue Goat.

"What's that smell?" she asked.

"Mash," said Shadrach with no further explanation. He lowered himself back into his seat at the table. They had obviously caught him in the middle of his meal. "Make yourselves at home. My humble abode," he said, waving a paw about. "Nothing to boast about, but it does for me. You kids hungry?"

"Yes!" cried Monk.

"Monk," Benny muttered. "Don't be rude."

"Not rude at all, my boy," said Shadrach. "A rat needs to eat, Lord knows. Now, you travel down that hallway there and take a right at the end. I dug myself a tunnel that runs directly to the Ratomat."

"What's a Ratomat?" asked Ella.

"You ask a lot of questions, don't you, missy?" Shadrach tilted his head back. Nobody spoke. They were mesmerized by the way his lips coaxed the curly peel of an apple into his cavernous mouth. "Switch has sent me some real barnyard bumpkins. But the old hoofer has been gone from the city awhile. Bet he doesn't even know about the Ratomat. It's a feeding station. We've got one on every block now. Up above, the humans drop things everywhere, and we used to have to forage for ourselves, one rat fighting with another over the scraps. But this new administration has upgraded the system. We have designated foragers. We call them DFs. Teams are assigned to different sections of the city. They channel the throwaways from the street drains and subway grates aboveground directly into the

Ratomat. You can see the food as it moves by in troughs, and you simply open the door and take what you want."

Monk had scuttled down the hallway before anybody could stop him, and the other three almost tripped over their own tails in their rush to catch up. Benny was hungry too, but he hesitated.

"Oh, go on with yourself," Shadrach said with a wave of his paw. "Plenty of time to talk once you've eaten."

Benny didn't wait another minute but took off after Ella and his brothers. They returned some time later, their trays loaded down with all sorts of delicacies. Benny had cautioned them to hold back, but he could see it was hopeless. Even he had not been able to resist so many new smells and taste sensations, from the exquisitely blackened banana peel to the delicate green mold on that pancake Switchtail had called a pizza. The five settled down around Shadrach's table and began to eat. They ate and they ate.

Finally Ella was full. "Why do the humans throw away so much food?" she asked.

"That's the kind of question I've learned to save for the pearly gates, my dear," said Shadrach.

"What do you mean?"

"Any question that asks 'Why do the humans do what they do?' Most of what they do makes no sense to us. The entire population of the Hollow is fed by food humans throw away. And listen to this. You kids know perfectly well that a self-respecting rat cleans himself six times a day?"

They nodded.

"Humans once a day," he said. "Sometimes not even that often. Disgusting. And look around this place. It's totally furnished by the castoffs of humans. This chair, for instance." They stared at his rocker, which was a wonderful contraption fashioned from two shoehorns and a large wooden matchbox. "They are creating entire mountains out of perfectly useful items that they've suddenly decided to throw away. They even tear down some of their best buildings. Down here in Rat Hollow, we have an architectural rescue committee."

"What's that?" asked Woody.

"They record the destruction up above, and then one by one, we replace the buildings in the Hollow, scaled down to our size. Go out into the main waiting room right here in Ratrun Central. It's the old Penn Station from aboveground. And when you need to send some tailmail, you'll see our main post office is lifted brick by brick from the one they demolished down in City Hall Park." He put a paw over his eyes. "Don't get me started on humans," he wailed while the five rats wondered if he would ever stop.

With one last dramatic shudder, Shadrach seemed to recover his composure. He leaned back in his chair and studied them for a while without speaking.

"Switchtail tells me that you're dancers," he said at long last.

They all nodded enthusiastically, as most of their mouths were still too full for conversation. Monk gulped down the last of his orange peel. "Tap," he mumbled. "And jazz."

"We started with ballet," Ella called out. "Uncle Switchtail made us."

Shadrach was picking at his teeth with a silver needle. "Switch knows his business. Ballet is where you always begin."

"We don't mean to disturb you, Mr. Shadrach," Benny said, his stomach at last satisfied. "We just need some advice now that we've made it to the Hollow. We're eager to get right down to the Boom Boom Room—"

"It's closed," Shadrach said abruptly. "Till further notice. Renovations aboveground at you know where."

"You mean the Crystal?" asked Ella.

"That's right. I see you know some history, then. So the owners of the Boom Boom Room decided to take a vacation. Hopped a train to Florida."

"For how long?" squeaked Fletcher.

Shadrach shrugged. "With that pack of lazy know-nothings, I couldn't tell you. They go when they want, come back when they feel like it. Not like the old days."

There was a solemn silence around the table. Woody's maggoty hot dog sat like a lump in his throat. Fletcher had to whack him twice between the shoulders to dislodge it. For once, Ella had nothing to say. They had come all this way to discover there was no Boom Boom Room. What were they supposed to do now?

7

MASH TIME

"My heavens," said Shadrach with a scrape of his chair. "What a sad collection of snouts. It's enough to give a rat indigestion. This calls for a round of mash." With some difficulty, he lifted himself out of his seat and stumbled into the back room.

Benny noticed that their host was blessed with a considerable girth. Switchtail had told them that Shadrach was once the most famous rat tapper in town, a permanent fixture at the Boom Boom Room. "He became a little too fond of the mash," Switchtail said. "Had a lady friend who lived up near the brewery, and she and her ratafia recipe turned out to be an irresistible temptation for old Shad." He put up his paw to stop Ella's question. "I know what you're going to ask. Ratafia is an especially delicious brew mixing brandy and almonds. Fries the brain and saps the energy of the strongest rodent. Age and liquor brought old Shad down, and when he finally left the profession, he wasn't dancing with anything but a broom and a mop."

"What do you mean?" Benny had asked.

"He ended his career at the Room as the janitor. The owners had to let him go because he slept more than he swept. But in his day," Switchtail had explained, "that rat was the king of shoe music."

The old king reappeared with a jug and six gleaming cups. "This is an important occasion, the arrival of you Rattoons, so I'm using my golden thimbles," he announced as he arranged them on the table. "Took me almost twenty years of scavenging to get a complete set. Of course, that was in the old days. Now the wares are displayed on tables at the regular weekend markets. Better selection thanks to our licensed scavengers but not half as much fun, I'll tell you."

Benny gave the group one of his fiercest looks. They had already eaten far more than their fill. From what Switchtail had told him about mash, this could be their undoing. Fletcher and Woody nodded, but Ella was busy raising her thimble in a toast, and Monk refused to catch his big brother's eye.

"To the Rattoons!" Shadrach boomed. He downed his drink in one gulp and immediately refilled his thimble.

"To our parents," Monk cried. He leapt up and raised his thimble high. "The roots of the Rattoons."

They all drank to that, but while Fletcher and Woody sipped and Benny only sniffed, Monk tipped back his head and opened his throat.

"Thatta rat," said Shadrach with relish. "A refill?"

"Sir," Benny started to say. "I think not—"

"You bet," said Monk, and shoved his thimble forward. Ella waved her paw weakly, but Shadrach ignored it.

They drank to Switchtail and a number of former dance favorites of Shadrach's. They drank to the present administration of the Hollow and the brilliance of the Ratomat. They drank to the Rattoons' success at the Boom Boom Room. Finally Mr. Shadrach began to tire of the constant refilling of the thimbles and wrapped his lips directly around the spout of the mash barrel itself. Benny watched this entire performance with horror. Ella's eyes had begun to roll about in her head in an alarming manner, while Monk was starting to show Shadrach his favorite tap steps, which involved a great deal of shuffling around in a circle. Finally, he sank to the floor in the middle of a muddled plié and tipped over on his side. But Shadrach drank on. Halfway through the second barrel of mash, he began to sing off-color ditties he'd learned from the ship rats down at the harbor joints. Suddenly there came a pounding on the door.

"Pipe down, Shadrach," cried a voice, "or I'll put you back in the slammer."

"You do that, Eddie, my boy. You just try that," Shadrach roared back. And he began to sing again. "Running up and down that rat line, chasing my baby, she's so fine. . . ." The hammering came again.

With a word from Benny, Woody and Fletcher jumped their host and the three of them managed to wrestle him into his cozy green nest in the back of the room. He put up little resistance and was snoring loudly by the time they rolled off him.

Benny opened the front door and stuck his snout outside. "Sorry for the noise, Mr. Eddie," he said to a large uniformed rat with a cudgel in his paw.

"Who are you?"

"I'm Benny, one of the Rattoons. We've come from the country to visit Mr. Shadrach. He was just trying to make us feel at home. It won't happen again."

"Yes, it will, young rat. It happens every single day."

"He's sleeping now."

"Well, that will give us all a few hours of peace and quiet. Except for the snoring. You'd better go back where you came from, Master Benny Rattoon. Shadrach's burrow is no place for a young country rat like yourself. Good evening to you, then."

"Good night, sir," said Benny. He shut the front door and drew the bolt across.

○   •   ○   •   ○

Shadrach slept the rest of that night and much of the next day. Monk woke moaning sometime in the night, but the rest ignored him. Teach him a lesson, Benny thought. When they made their way down the tunnel to the Rato-mat the next morning, Ella pretended to be full, but they all knew she had a terrible ache in her belly. Monk didn't move at all until they picked him up by his tail and gave him a stern shake.

"My head," he cried. "It's going to fall off."

"Serves you right," said Fletcher.

"Pull yourself together," Benny said. "We're moving on. This is no place for us."

They looked over at Shadrach, who, to their alarm, opened his right eye. "What's that?" he said, making vain efforts to rouse himself. "What did you say?"

"Well, Mr. Shadrach, we thank you very much for your hospitality, but we think we shouldn't trouble you anymore," Fletcher said. "So we'll be moving along."

"Now, this isn't good at all," muttered Shadrach, who had managed to prop himself up in a sitting position. "I believe I got a little carried away last night. If Switchtail hears of this, he'll be angry. Oh, dear, I've made a mess of things again, it seems." He went on mumbling to himself and scratching his belly in a worried way. The blustering, mash-swilling rat of the night before had been replaced by a worried old rodent with drooping whiskers and a dusting of bread crumbs trapped in his shoulder fur. Benny stepped forward.

"Mr. Shadrach, we can't wait for the Boom Boom Room to open again. We need to start our dancing career now. So what do you suggest?"

Shadrach studied them for a long time, but with such an unfocused gaze that they thought maybe he'd managed to go back to sleep with his eyes open.

"Mr. Shadrach, wake up. Did you hear what Benny said?" Ella demanded.

The old rat covered his ears. "Not so loud, young lady. There's a complete drum set working in my head already. I heard your brother. I'm thinking. Frankly, you're a bunch of amateurs. Only place for you to start is the platform."

"What platform?" asked Monk from a corner of the room. His legs had given way, and he'd slid quietly down the wall when nobody was looking.

"Out there," Shadrach said with a jerk of his head. The abrupt movement made him moan in pain. He massaged his temples with both paws. "The train platform. Set your-selves up at the south end around four o'clock. Those com-muter rats always got time for a little shoe music. Word'll spread 'bout the new act in town. The managers from the clubs will come sniffing around. Why, I know a rat tapper who—" But suddenly something seemed to pull the old rat's plug, and he sank back down into his nest without another word. In a matter of minutes, he was snoring again.

Monk was the last one out. "See you later, Mr. Shadrach."

The large mountain of rat didn't move so much as a whisker in response.

8

THE ACROBRAT*S*

The Rattoons made their way through the sparse midafternoon crowd to the south end of the platform. Fletcher handed out their tap shoes while Woody set up the boom box behind a pillar.

"You kids better move along," said a passing rat in a lab coat. "Not much time left."

"What are you talking about?" Woody asked. "We're performing here at four."

"Stick around," Fletcher said. "You'll be amazed."

"If *you* stick around, you'll be flattened," said the rat amiably. "You're on the Brats' territory."

"Who are the Brats?" asked Ella.

The rat pulled his eyeglasses down and peered at them for a moment. "Country rats," he said to himself. "Must be. There's nobody in the Hollow who doesn't know the Brats. The Acrobrats. Black ship rats who brought their act over last year," he explained. "They're the hit of the town. They set up here at four-thirty every day. You all better be history by then." With a shrug he trotted off, calling to the conductor to hold his train.

∘　•　∘　•　∘

A crowd did start to gather soon after four and stared curiously at the Rattoons doing one of their combinations. Then from the back someone cried out, "They're coming. Make room, you rats up front. Make room for the Acrobrats."

Above the commotion, a banner swaying from two poles announced the arrival of the stupendous, unique, one-of-a-kind aerial artists, the Acrobrats.

Three slim black rats in striped satin vests and gaily colored tights came to a halt in front of the dance line. They looked at one another and then back at the Rattoons.

"Who are you?" asked one of the Brats, whose carefully waxed whiskers extended backward to the top of his ears. The aerialists were backed by a gang of four tough-looking roustabouts in caps that were cocked low over their mean, glittering eyes.

"Well, sir," Benny said, stumbling forward. "We are a jazz and tap group called the Rattoons and—"

"*Rattus norvegicus,*" said the shortest Brat to his two compatriots.

"What else?" snorted the whiskered one. "Lowbellies. Barnyard browns."

"We are not brown, we're gray," Woody said. "Mostly."

"Well, what are *you*?" Ella cried.

They swiveled as if on cue and eyed her with ill-disguised contempt. They might as well have been looking at a bug trapped under one of their paws.

"Uneducated female," remarked the third Brat with a tap of his cane on the platform. He removed his top hat and carefully wiped the spotless rim with a turn of his costumed elbow.

"We, my dear lady, are the superior race," he said. "*Rattus rattus*. Otherwise known as the black rats, the ship rats, the roof rats. You hug the ground. We were born to fly through the air. Now, if you lowbellies would be so kind as to move aside, we'll show you just what we can do. Frankly, if you don't get out of the way and be quick about it, I'm afraid you might be in some danger. Our loyal fans here have been known to get quite rowdy."

This remark drew a roar of laughter from the crowd.

"We want the Brats," they cried. "Move on, you barnyard babies."

Woody bundled up the boom box without another word. At a sign from Benny, the Rattoons moved off to the side but held their ground in the front row. They were eager to see what all the fuss was about.

The roustabouts flipped their caps around and set to work, hoisting the high poles with the two swinging bars. Halfway up the poles, they strung a wire from end to end. Meanwhile the Brats set aside their capes, canes, and hats. They began to stretch their limbs and wrap their wrists.

"Ladies and gentlerats," announced one of the rousters. "Without further ado, I give you the Acrobrats."

The crowd roared and the three bespangled rats separated, two to one pole and one to the other. With lightning speed, they scampered up the hoist lines. One of them stopped at the wire while the other two went all the way up to the platforms at the very top of the poles.

"On the first trapeze," crowed the announcer, "Alfredo the Twisting Triple." The rat who had looked at Ella with such disdain gave an elaborate bow and leapt into the air, his belly plastered to the trapeze. He appeared to slip, and the crowd gasped in horror. Then, at the last minute, he caught himself with a quick wrap of his tail around the bar. He spread his paws and arched his back while urging the trapeze higher and higher into the dark recesses of the ceiling above the train platform.

"Now, please put your paws together for Lalo, the one and only, world-renowned Tail Catcher."

The tallest rat lifted the other trapeze from its hook, settled himself on it like a child on a swing, and with perfect timing swung out to meet Alfredo. The roustabouts flicked on two spotlights. All eyes below tipped upward. All heads swayed back and forth, hypnotized by the rhythm of the two fliers.

"And finally, last but not least, Arturo the Flying Wire Walker."

The crowd whooped and cheered as Arturo, the smallest of the three, touched a delicately pointed paw to the wire and tripped across first on his back legs and then again only on his front. He danced up the pole to the tiny platform at the top and blew a kiss to the audience.

Alfredo swung out one more time and then leapt from his bar, turned a double layout, and was caught by Lalo's tail. The two rats swung back and forth, back and forth until Alfredo curled up and threw himself back at the bar that Arturo had tossed his way at just the right moment.

Fletcher nudged Woody. "I think we'd better take the train home," he whispered. "Nobody cares about a bunch of tappers when they can see this."

Woody didn't answer. Like the rest of the mesmerized crowd, he couldn't take his eyes off the three fliers as they traced their way across the lights. Who needed music or tap shoes or the ground at all when you could take to the air like a bird and defy the laws of gravity?

The announcer was speaking again. "And now, ladies and gentlerats, I call to you for silence. The Acrobrats will be performing the most difficult part of their act. Alfredo will turn for you the famous triple *salto mortale*! The somersault of death. Please note there is no net to save him. Stand back. He has informed me that no matter what happens to him, he wishes no harm to come to any of you."

The hushed crowd made more room. The crew of the 5:34 bound for Whisker Tunnel had delayed its departure.

Passengers were leaning out the windows, their snouts tilted upward.

"What's a *salto mortale*?" Monk whispered to the rat standing next to him. The young female did not turn her head when she spoke. "The triple somersault," she said through pursed lips. "Alfredo is the only rat who has turned the triple and lived to tell the tale. His cousin Ernesto broke his neck attempting it."

"Shhh," whispered a thick brown rat in overalls from behind them. "Alfredo needs silence."

There was a drumroll from a roustabout with a bucket between his knees, and the spotlights found the three performers. First Lalo, the catcher, pushed off and began his long arc back and forth. Then Alfredo, with a solemn nod to the hushed crowd, leapt onto the second bar with limbs outstretched. At the top of the upswing, he threw his body into the air with such ferocity that his tail curled right up along his back to his ears. The crowd sucked in its breath and held it.

"One revolution," called the announcer, "two . . . and THREE." He ended with a roar as Lalo caught Alfredo with one flick of his thick tail around his partner's chest. They swung together like that for what seemed like ages until, with a grunt, Arturo threw Alfredo his trapeze, and, with a last full-twisting somersault in midair, Alfredo caught the bar and sailed it smoothly back to join Arturo on his platform.

The crowd went wild. Strangers pummeled one another on the back, calling Alfredo's name and raising their paws in salute. Overcome with emotion, the conductor opened and closed the doors over and over again so it seemed as if the train itself were applauding Alfredo's death-defying triple.

9

MOVING ON

The Whisker Tunnel express closed its doors one last time and pulled out of the station. Rats picked up their briefcases and newspapers and tried to find their way back to their everyday, earthbound lives. The roustabouts dismantled the poles and packed away the rest of the gear while the three Acrobrats stood in a circle, signing autographs for an eager crowd of young rats.

"Benny, we'd better go," Woody said.

Benny shook his head. "I want to talk to them." He had such a fierce expression on his face that not one of his siblings questioned him.

The Acrobrats fastened their capes and began to move off down the platform as Benny stepped forward from behind a pillar. "Excuse me, sirs."

"Who are you?" asked Alfredo. "We're not signing any more autographs."

"My name is Benny, and this is—"

"Why, it's the lowbellies," said Lalo with a dismissive wave of his paw. "So did you enjoy the show?"

"It was spectacular," cried Monk.

"We'd like your advice, sir," Benny pressed on in his solemn voice.

"Give them the info, Arturo," Alfredo said. "And let's be on our way. The triple always makes me thirsty."

The Acrobrats swept past as Benny stood staring at the business card that had been pressed into his paw. AERIAL ARTISTES FLYING SCHOOL, it read. APPLICATIONS ACCEPTED YEAR-ROUND, with an address.

Benny ran after them with the other Rattoons trailing behind. "Mr. Alfredo, sir," he said, scooting once more in front of the black rat. "That's not what I mean."

The Acrobrats came to a halt. "I have to say, young rat, you are beginning to irritate me," Alfredo muttered. "What on earth do you want?"

"We've just arrived in the Hollow. We are great tap dancers, and we came here to perform at the Boom Boom Room, but it's closed and the train platform is your territory. So where should we go?"

The three Brats looked at one another. Woody remembered that look later, and he wondered if they hadn't passed some secret signal among themselves.

"Only one place for beginners," Alfredo said as his eye swept across the five of them. "We made our start there. The steps of the Metropolitan Museum. The crowd is constant, so you don't have to worry about catching the rush hour. You set up about three in the afternoon."

"And they're an enthusiastic bunch," said Lalo. "They like some live entertainment after all that dead art on the walls."

"Yes, you'll do well there," Arturo added.

"Where is it?" Benny asked.

The three Brats jerked their heads upward with one syncopated motion.

"Up there?" squeaked Monk. "Aboveground?"

"That's right. You're not scared to go aboveground, are you?" Alfredo asked, his nose twitching close to Benny's as if he were sniffing out the smell of fear.

"Well, no, sir, we're not. Of course not."

"If you want to make a name for yourselves, you lowbellies, you'll have to take some risks. Poke those little snouts out of Rat Hollow. It'll do you good. There's a whole world out there just waiting to be conquered. We know. We've crossed the ocean countless times ourselves."

"What's an ocean?" Ella asked, but Benny tapped her on the head to silence her.

"Sir, how do we get there?" Monk was asking as he unrolled his map.

"Take the train to Central Depot and switch there for the Red Line," Lalo explained. "I see you got one of the old maps. Useful thing when you get aboveground. So you get off at Snout Park. There's a tail opener there at the north end of the station. It comes out in the fountain right in front of the museum."

"You Norways are good swimmers, from what I understand," Arturo said.

"The ducks taught us," Ella announced. The three fliers stared at her as if she had suddenly said something in a foreign tongue. "Down at the barnyard," she added in a smaller voice.

Woody pinched her. Her voice drifted into silence.

"And if you happen to meet up with our old friend Oliver, do give him our best," said Lalo. But his voice was sarcastic, and he spoke through clenched teeth.

"You mean Oliver String Bean Bailey?" Benny asked.

"The very one," said Arturo.

"You know Oliver Bailey?" asked Ella.

But Alfredo wasn't listening. He was already striding down the platform, and the others hurried to catch up. "Good luck to you," he called back with a wave of his paw. "We'll be looking for your name in lights." The echo of his voice lingered in the dim recesses of the cavernous ceiling, where not so long ago he had flown through the air over the heads of his adoring fans.

He's taunting us, Benny thought. He doesn't think we can do it.

○　●　○　●　○

As soon as the Acrobrats were out of hearing, everybody began to talk at once.

"Switchtail said we were never to go aboveground—"

"What would he think of this—"

"It's too dangerous; we won't ever come back—"

"How do they know Oliver Bailey?"

Benny put up his paw for silence.

"It's time we started to make decisions for ourselves," he said. "Switchtail hasn't been to the city in years. Things have changed."

"But he said—," Ella started.

"I'm not finished," Benny said, and there was an authority in his voice that they had not heard before. "Remember that Switch sent us to Shadrach. And what good did he do us, I'd like to know?"

"He taught us about the Ratomat," Monk squeaked.

"And the mash barrel," Benny reminded him. Monk stared at the ground while on either side Fletcher and Woody each dug an elbow into his ribs.

"Any rat on the street could have told us about the Ratomat," Benny went on. "Now, I'm sure Shadrach was a remarkable tapper in his time, but those days are over. We need to start thinking for ourselves."

"So we won't go back to Shadrach's tonight?" Ella asked.

"No, we won't. We will make our way to this museum immediately. Monk, you're the navigator. Time to do your job."

The other rats stole nervous looks at one another, but the determined expression on their older brother's face convinced them any further objections would be useless.

10

THE FOUNTAIN

The trains in Rat Hollow ran on rubber wheels scavenged from the discarded toys of human children, so the rides were smooth and silent. Monk did his job well. It seemed that in no time at all, they had found their way to the tail opener at the north end of Snout Park Station.

They bunched up behind Benny, who felt their anxious breath on his back.

"Now, remember," he said, "we'll be coming up into a fountain, so you've got to be ready to swim. It won't be much bigger than the duck pond."

"Benny," Woody said.

"What?"

"I'm scared."

"So am I," Benny said. "But we don't have any other choice. We've got to do this. Ready?"

"Ready," Ella squeaked.

Benny poked the tip of his tail into the hole, and the door swung open. The five slipped through quickly into a dark tunnel that smelled of water. A trickle ran by their feet, and slowly the water moved up over their waists and then they were swimming, following Benny, who was fighting the current to the top. His head popped out first, and then the other four came up, gasping for air. But the moment they surfaced, it seemed as if somebody had dumped a bucket full of water on their heads and the pressure forced them back under. Benny surfaced once more and managed to take a quick breath before the cascading plumes pushed him down again. Underwater, he motioned to the others to follow him to the edge of the pond.

One by one they scrabbled over the first low stone wall to the calmer waters out of range of the fountain. At last they bumped up against the outer wall and dragged themselves over. Benny lifted his head and counted only three sodden shivering heaps on the pavement.

"Monk," he squealed in horror. "Where's Monk?"

They struggled to a sitting position and looked around.

"Fletcher, Ella, back in the water with me," Benny commanded. "Woody, wait here and watch. He may come up at the other end."

With their paws outstretched, the three rats began a systematic search of the slimy, sloping floor. Every so often one would bob to the surface and check with Woody, who was nervously patrolling the edge, one eye on the fountain and the other on the clumps of humans strolling down the dark avenue. Nobody had spied them yet, but he was sure it was only a matter of time.

Ella came up sputtering. "Here," she cried before she dove again. Fletcher went in after her and beckoned underwater to Benny.

Monk was unconscious. It took two of them to get him to the surface while Ella struggled with the map tube. They dragged Monk over both stone walls and onto the pavement. Benny began trying to revive him with short quick thrusts to his upper belly while the others stood around gasping for air. Their brother did not move.

"Is he, is he—," Woody started to ask, but he didn't dare finish the question.

Benny shook his head, refusing to entertain the awful thought.

"Benny, don't kill him," whispered Ella. "You're pushing so hard." Just at that moment, Monk's mouth opened and a spume of water shot straight up into the air and drenched Benny all over again. Monk began to cough and sputter as another wave of water washed out of his belly.

"Hey, Monk," Fletcher cried. "You've turned into a fountain." They laughed weakly while their brother sat up and looked around.

"It was the map tube," he croaked. "It got tangled around my neck."

"It's all right now," Benny said in a calming voice. "Ella got it."

"I knew I couldn't lose it," Monk said.

"You were right," Benny said with a clumsy pat on his brother's damp head.

"Benny," Woody said. "We'd better clear out of here quick."

He pointed his snout toward a pack of rowdy human teenagers on rolling boards who were beginning to converge on the plaza around the fountain.

Supporting Monk between them, the damp rats gathered up their belongings and crept as unobtrusively as possible toward one of the lower entrances to the museum. Halfway there, they veered around a grate that seemed to lead belowground. Benny hesitated for a minute. The space between the struts looked wide enough to push through the wardrobe suitcase and the backpack. This might be a place to spend the night.

Suddenly they heard a shout, accompanied by a slap of skateboard wheels against the pavement behind them.

"Josh," one kid yelled to another. "What's that?"

"Looks like a bunch of animals."

"Run," yelled Benny. But, what with the backpack and the suitcase and Monk limping, running was out of the question. They hobbled and scrabbled along and ducked through the large metal door to the museum just as a security guard with a bunch of keys came around the corner from the other end of the hallway.

"Hey," he yelled, "what are you kids doing?"

"Following them," one boy said. "We think they're rats."

"Following who?" the guard said.

The five flattened themselves against a shadowed wall.

"I can't see them anymore," said the boy. "But I know they went in here."

"Turn on the lights and we'll show you," said another. "You don't want a lot of rats in the museum, do you?"

"What I don't want is a bunch of kids on skateboards," said the guard. "Now, scram." He shooed them out and locked the door before he scanned the hallway. The rats, who had relaxed for a moment, sucked in their bellies and played statue.

"Kids," he muttered to himself, and plodded back down the hallway, swinging his keys. The five rats heard them chink and jingle, loud at first. Then softer. Then—silence.

11

THE MUSEUM AT NIGHT

In the museum, the guards seemed to turn up with no warning in the most surprising places. Three times, just as the group had settled down for the night, they had to pull themselves together and slide away through a darkened gallery or down another hallway filled with statues of naked humans. Benny was beginning to wonder whether this whole idea had been wise, and he knew Ella and Woody were thinking the same thing. Monk was too bedraggled to think about anything. Whenever they had to move again, he picked himself up and followed along like a sleepwalker. Fletcher had taken to reading the labels.

"Look at this," he cried as they tiptoed through something called the Greek and Roman wing. They hushed him into a whisper. "This statue was carved in 1300 B.C."

"What's *beesee*?" Ella asked in a weary voice.

"Must be sometime long ago," said Fletcher. "Poor guy is missing one arm and the other is hung up in a sling."

Finally Benny settled them down in a place where a circle of tall statues smiled genially down on them. It was odd that some of the human forms seemed to have sprouted four or five arms and one head looked more animal than human, but Benny was simply too tired to worry about details. Woody set the boom box up in front of a wall vent in case it needed drying out.

"I'll take it apart tomorrow," he mumbled. "After I sleep."

The four of them curled into a cozy, damp tangle underneath a radiator.

"Come on, Fletcher," Ella called. "Time to sleep."

"I'm not tired," he whispered. "Think I'll look around."

"See if you can find some food," Benny said in a slurred voice. "Don't get lost," he added, and fell asleep as soon as the sentence was out of his mouth.

Food was a good idea, Fletcher thought as he made his way down the wide front steps. He couldn't remember the last time they had eaten. Although his nose was not as reliable as Monk's, it didn't take him long to find his way to the main cafeteria. The place was locked up tight and, sad to say, clean as a whistle. He was only able to nose one small cookie fragment and a grape out from under a corner table. These he ate with guilt, thinking of his hungry siblings under the radiator upstairs. Never mind, he thought. Tomorrow when the humans come back, there will be plenty for all of us.

It was on the way back upstairs that he began to pay more attention to the contents of the cabinets. He skittered along the moldings, peering through the glass to read the labels. The Rattoons made a kind of art with their feet, he thought, but the moment the song was finished, the dance was done. This art was made with hands, not feet, and the humans saved it through all the years. They built this enormous building so thousands of eyes could come and stare at it—and Fletcher could see why. Each artist was recording the way the world looked in his time. Trees, clouds, flowers, humans, of course. And animals. The more Fletcher looked, the more animals he saw. There were rabbits and owls and geese and deer and horses and water buffalo and tigers and gazelles and yaks and ibexes and camels. He leapt from case to case, searching eagerly for his first glimpse of a rat. Rats had been around in ancient times. He knew that from the stories his father had told him.

In one room, he found an entire barnyard fashioned from clay figures. A pig was wallowing around in his sty. Goats milled about in a pen. Ducks floated in a pond. Surely he would find a rat here. Barnyards always had rats. But no, not a one.

He roamed farther afield. One case held nothing but animals, most of them killing one another. A lion was eating a doe. Two dogs were attacking a stag. A horse was trying to fight another lion who had leapt on his back. But no rats. No rats anywhere.

By the time he limped back down the vast marble hallways to the tangle of sleeping siblings, he had worked himself into a fury.

"There are no rats," he said in a voice loud enough to wake the dead.

His family popped up all at once.

"I can't breathe," Woody squealed. He'd been dreaming he was trapped under a waterfall with the boom box tied around his feet.

"Yes, you can," said Ella. "Open your eyes. Now, what's wrong with you, Fletcher?"

"There is not a single rat anywhere in this museum," Fletcher announced in a great booming voice that seemed to racket around the walls like a flying animal.

"Be quiet, Fletcher," Benny warned.

"I will not be quiet," Fletcher boomed again. "I am outraged. These humans have put every single animal into their art except for our noble species. There are jaguars and goats and carvings of lions on earrings and stone elephants and paintings of cats chasing butterflies and spiders. Of all things—" He was spluttering now. "Have you ever heard of a cat chasing a butterfly instead of a rat?"

Benny stood up and shook his brother. "Get ahold of yourself," he said in a steely voice.

"We are nothing but vermin to them, rodents to be trapped and baited and hounded down all our days. I demand that we leave this place at once. I will not rest one more night in these halls—"

"You haven't rested one minute in these halls so far," said Ella. "And thanks to you, we haven't done too much resting either."

But nothing could stop Fletcher. "—where our entire history has been ignored, where we are considered nothing but vermin, lower than a snake's belly—" Three of them wrestled him to the ground and held him there until his voice slowed to an unintelligible mumble and finally into silence.

"He's gone to sleep," Monk said.

"It's too much strain for him," Benny murmured. "For all of us. It's my fault. We should never have left Rat Hollow. I don't know why I believed those Acrobrats."

They heard the now familiar jangle of a guard's keys and scuttled back under the radiator. Two shiny black shoes squeaked past and came to rest directly in front of their nesting place. A chunk of leather had been gouged out of the right toe.

"I don't hear nothin', Joe," called someone from another room.

"It was in here. Some kind of talking, almost." Joe flicked on his flashlight. "Now, what the devil is that?"

Ella reached over and very carefully pulled in the tip of Fletcher's tail.

"It moved."

The other man squeaked through the gallery to join the one called Joe. Fletcher stirred in his sleep, and Ella covered his mouth with a paw. Four Rattoons sat in a tense row just inches from four thick-soled shoes.

"What moved?" asked the first voice.

"I don't know, Frank. A worm or a string or something."

"Well, point your flashlight under there and look."

"I don't like crawling things."

"Oh, jeez," said Frank. "Give me the stupid flashlight."

"On the count of three," Benny whispered. "We're going to make a run for it. Right over their shoes, up their pant legs. Scare them half to death."

Woody picked up the boom box. Ella shook Fletcher awake and whispered the plan in his ear.

"Whaddya know?" said Joe. "Flashlight went off. Just like that."

"Give it here."

"What about yours?" Joe snapped.

"Don't have one."

"You're on duty without a flashlight, Frank. You could get sacked for that."

Joe was making his way into the next room. Frank followed. "You're not gonna report me, are you?" he asked. "Stupid little thing like that."

The rats' breathing slowed down.

"Well, I guess not. So long as you don't tell nobody how I am about crawling things."

They passed out of earshot.

"His flashlight didn't go out," Ella said with a snort. "He was just plain scared of Fletcher's tail and what it might be connected to."

"I don't care what he was scared of," said Benny, settling back down. "As long as we don't have to move again. Fletcher's already asleep. Do you think the rest of you could pipe down? We've got a long day ahead."

Nobody said another word.

12

BREAKFAST

 **B**enny sat up with a start. He'd been woken by a loud growling noise. He braced himself and waited. There, it came again. Directly from Ella's stomach, which had been his pillow.

Woody was the only one up. "The boom box is dry as a bone," he reported in a whisper. "I checked it inside and out. Switch said it was waterproof, but I didn't believe him. And I unrolled the maps. They're pretty dry too."

"We've got to get moving," Benny said. He shook the rest of them awake. "Time to get some food into our bellies."

"What about the Ratomat?" Monk said brightly.

They glared at him.

"Aboveground?" Ella asked.

"Forgot," Monk mumbled.

"Cheer up," said Fletcher. "Last night in my travels, I found the cafeteria. It won't be the Ratomat, but there should be a few scraps we can nibble on. You know humans. They may not put us in their paintings, but they do manage to feed us even when they don't mean to."

With Fletcher in the lead, they made their way down a set of back stairs behind the bookstore and crept back through the Greek and Roman galleries, dodging the occasional guard. Fletcher gave a running commentary the whole way, mostly on the subject of the wide range of animals that these revolting humans had chosen to portray in their art.

"We should have put blinders on him," Woody whispered to Benny, who nodded wearily as Fletcher screeched to an abrupt halt one more time and started another lecture.

"Fletcher," Ella said in an extravagantly patient voice. "Right now we're hungry and you have a job to do."

"I do?"

"You're leading us to the cafeteria. So let's go."

"All right, all right," he said. "But it doesn't hurt to do a little sight-seeing on the way."

"Fletcher," Benny said.

"Fine, follow me. But I've never known such a bunch of see-nothing rats in my life."

They didn't argue. It would have been a waste of time.

When they finally reached the cafeteria, it was deserted. The kitchen was shuttered, the chairs all tipped up against the tables.

"Fletcher," said Ella. "What's going on?"

"I guess it's not open yet. We'll just have to wait."

Monk lifted his snout to the air. "I smell something," he said. "In that direction."

When it came to food, they knew Monk's nose could be trusted, so they turned on their paws and followed his lead without argument.

They passed through something called the Egyptian wing. Fletcher began reading the labels again.

"Oxen," he spat. "Jackals. Cranes. The odd cat, even. Animals to the left of you, animals to the right of you, but nary a rat to be seen."

By this time no one was paying any attention to him. Their noses had caught up with Monk's. Somebody was cooking something, and it was getting closer.

"It's there," Woody said, pointing down a set of stairs.

"Let's go," cried Monk. He hopped onto the top step, but something strange happened to his legs. They didn't take him where he wanted to go. He was running twice as fast just to stay in one place. Finally he gave up and got off. "What a peculiar staircase," he said.

They ducked out of sight as a guard stepped on the bottom step and floated up toward them without moving his legs at all.

"He smells of bacon," Monk said as the man passed by without noticing the little clutch of rats.

"The food's definitely down there," Ella said. "But how do we get to it?"

"There's another staircase on the other side," Fletcher explained.

"Well, for rat's sake, why didn't you tell us?" Benny said.

"Nobody asked," Fletcher answered as he led them back out into the Egyptian gallery and around another corner. "And you four haven't exactly been listening to me either."

"Sometimes, Fletch—," Woody muttered, but nobody heard the rest of his sentence as they scampered down a perfectly normal set of stairs that didn't move at all. They squeezed under the doors and peeked into a large, noisy room.

No wonder so few guards were out and about at this hour. They were all down here. A gaggle of them were gathered around a table. One man was snoring loudly, his forehead on a place mat, while the rest were sitting in silence, shoveling in breakfast.

The Rattoons slipped under the table and stationed themselves in a circle, each between two human legs. Woody pointed to the shoes he stood between, and Ella nodded. The toe of the right one had a gouge in it, which meant that unbeknownst to him, Joe, the guard who hated crawling things, was sitting right on top of a passel of rats. Woody only hoped he was a slovenly eater.

It turned out to be slim pickings, a disappointment after the luxuries of the Ratomat. The humans were hungry, and since they kept their mouths only inches from their food, very little slipped between fork and lip. Monk got a chunk of scrambled egg, and the five of them split a piece of toast crust that slid off somebody's plate, but Woody got drenched when Joe knocked over his lukewarm coffee with a sudden jerk of his elbow. There was a great deal of cursing and fuming, although luckily nobody seemed inclined to drop to the floor and clean up the mess.

They had a little more success when they moved into the kitchen itself. The cook was in a jubilant mood, and he was flinging the flapjacks up in the air more like a juggler twirling plates than a short-order chef. His assistant was giggling helplessly, and when one of the cakes sailed off the spatula into a corner of the kitchen, the two of them looked at each other, shrugged, and then went right on mixing and flipping as if nothing had happened. Benny and Woody dragged the warm pancake into a dusty corner of the storeroom. The Rattoons munched happily from the outside toward the center until they were nose to nose and their bellies at last were full.

The rats could sense the movement of more humans through the space above them. They grabbed a ride on the floating staircase and then Monk, who did have the best sense of direction, led the troop through some back galleries and down another set of stairs, dodging staff and guards the whole way.

Finally the Rattoons found themselves in the back of an enormous coatroom. They hunkered down behind a baby stroller that looked as if it had been parked there some months before. Spiders had woven webs between the spokes of the wheels.

"Now what?" Ella asked.

"We don't want to start our performance until the afternoon, when the crowds pick up, but I think I've figured out a place for us to spend the day," Benny said.

"What's wrong with this place?" Woody asked.

"No good. Too much human traffic here."

He poked his nose between the wheels of the stroller and cased the joint.

"All right," he whispered. "We've got to go now. Hug the wall. Try to stay in the shadows. If I stop, everybody freeze. Ready?"

"Are we leaving the museum?" Fletcher asked, a plaintive note in his voice.

"We are. It's too dangerous."

"But there's so much more to see. I read a story somewhere about an elephant god that was carried around on the back of a rat. And what about those old rugs hanging on the walls? I bet they stitched a rat into one of those—"

"Fletch, stuff it," said Woody. "We don't have time. Go on, Benny. We'll follow you."

Without another word, Benny slipped out from between the wheels of the stroller and slunk along the wall, his siblings tight behind him. The two checkout clerks were bent over the newspaper and never noticed a strangely shaped shadow gliding along the marble molding under the counter. The five made their way undisturbed down the dark hallway where they'd first entered and settled in the corner next to the doorway to wait for the official opening hour.

Soon a guard with a bunch of keys unlocked the door for a group of savvy visitors who were avoiding the long lines upstairs. Benny signaled, and the five slipped out as a large man with a thick accent began to argue with the guard about the ridiculous smoking rules in American museums.

Halfway across the plaza Fletcher slowed and called out, "My museum!" but Monk urged him on with regular sharp pokes of his snout between his shoulder blades.

"All right, I'm going, I'm going. But I'll be back, I promise you that," Fletcher muttered under his breath.

Suddenly with no warning, Benny disappeared up ahead of them. Then Woody and Ella. It looked as if the earth had simply swallowed them whole.

"Where did they go?" Monk whispered. He was keeping a nervous eye on a baby in a stroller who kept pointing in their direction and shrieking with delight or possibly horror. It was hard to tell with humans.

"Here," came a fierce whisper from under their feet. They looked down to see six eyes peering up at them through the grate of a catch basin. "Map tube first," Benny ordered, and Monk slid it through to their waiting paws.

"Come on, Fletcher, " Ella called. "No more art."

With one last mournful look over his shoulder, Fletcher lowered himself, followed immediately by Monk. Not a minute too soon either, Benny thought as the wheels of a hot-dog vendor's cart rumbled over them.

13

THE PERFORMANCE

Benny's hiding place was brilliant. A metal ladder led down from the grate, but next to it a square wire basket filled with dead leaves made a perfect nest for the weary rats. The people up above never seemed to look down through the grate, and even if they had, the dried-up leaves provided excellent camouflage for the barnyard browns, as Lalo had dubbed them.

Fletcher kept trying to poke his nose through the wire mesh of the grate to stare again at his museum. Twice Benny pulled him back before his snout was speared by a lady's stiletto heel.

"I thought you hated that place," Ella said grumpily.

"I haven't given up yet. Somewhere inside that building, I'm sure there's a picture of a rat," Fletcher declared. "I'm going to find it."

"Some other lifetime, Fletch," Woody sneered. "In this one, you're a dancer."

"A stiff, tired dancer like the rest of us," said Ella in a worried whisper. "We have to go out there and strut our stuff this afternoon with very little sleep and no rehearsal in days."

"Ella's right," Benny said. "We ought to be resting while we can. Close your eyes, the lot of you."

○　●　○　●　○

The day seemed to last forever. They dozed on and off, but their slumber was constantly interrupted by human noise. Babies squealed, buses honked, brakes shrieked, skateboards slapped against the pavement, and teenagers played some strange pounding sounds they called music.

Ella wanted to watch the passing parade, but she couldn't convince Benny to let her slip up above for a look, so she ran up and down the ladder over and over again to warm her muscles. Woody tested their music on the boom box. At the foot of the ladder, Fletcher draped their tuxedos in front of an active steam vent to get out the wrinkles. Monk spent time poring over his maps. Benny worried.

He kept thinking about the knowing look that had passed among the Acrobrats when they suggested aboveground. Why had he listened to them? This was a dangerous place. After all, Joe the guard had called them crawling things and he hadn't even laid eyes on them. Fletcher claimed humans considered them nothing but vermin.

How would those people ever get past their prejudices about rats and see the tapping of their paws, the rhythm they carried in their bodies, the songs that sang in their souls? Benny's spirits sank as the afternoon wore on.

"I think we need an escape route," he said to Monk in a low voice so as not to upset the others. "Just in case something goes wrong."

"I was thinking the same thing," Monk said. "I've been studying the aboveground side of the map." He jabbed at a place with his paw. "Right beyond the end of the museum is a big park."

"So if there's trouble, we head that way," said Benny. "What direction is that?"

"South," said Monk before he rolled up the maps and tucked them away in the carrying tube.

Fletcher handed out the costumes he had picked for their afternoon show. "Ella says we're doing a jazz routine today," he said. "The tap shoes will attract too much attention when we're crossing the plaza."

They climbed into their tuxedos, twirled their canes, and snapped out their top hats. Woody took them through the music selections, and Ella reminded them of the combinations.

Benny looked down the brave little row with pride.

"Benny," Ella said at last. "I think it's time now."

He pulled himself together. There was no turning back. No matter what, he wouldn't let them see how worried he was. After all, he was the leader, the one Switchtail had chosen to make the decisions.

"Right you are, Ella. So, are we all ready?"

Four heads nodded solemnly.

"For the moment, keep your hats flat. We need to do some maneuvering to get the best spot. Up we go."

The number of people moving through the plaza in every possible direction was a horrible shock. The five rats had never been so close to so many humans at one time. The smell and noise and sheer volume of their huge bodies almost drove Benny back into their hiding place.

But as usual, it seemed that the humans were intent on their own business. They barely noticed one another, never mind a pack of ankle-high rats. The five were able to scuttle in between the wheels of the hot dog cart without being seen. There Benny put up his paw.

"We're going to reconnoiter," he whispered.

"What's that?" Ella asked.

"Look around. Decide on our next move."

Monk pointed to a large crowd of humans gathered around something in front of the main steps. After a while, a group of them parted. A person dressed in white robes with a painted white face was cruising down the street with a strangely exaggerated walk.

"What's that?" asked Fletcher.

"It looks like one of the statues has come out of the museum," said Woody.

"It looks like a ghost," said Ella.

"It's a mime," Benny explained. "Switch told me about them. It's perfect. He's exactly what we need." And his spirits lifted for the first time all afternoon.

"What do you mean?" Monk whispered. Suddenly his voice rose to an agonized squeak. He pointed at his tail, trapped under a vendor's sneaker.

"Hold still," Ella said.

Monk nodded. The sneaker was lifted up, and just before it was put down again, Ella snatched Monk's tail away. She kissed it. "Better?" she said as she handed it to him. He nodded again and tucked it ever so carefully into the top of his pants.

"A mime," Benny said, "imitates others. He never speaks. His body is his instrument. If you watch carefully, you'll see. A woman walks down the street. She doesn't see him, but the crowd does. He walks along behind her. See? He's imitating her."

They heard the crowd burst into laughter. The woman looked around; the mime froze. She shrugged and walked on.

"Follow me. When I give the signal, Woody, you start the music. We'll fall into line right behind him."

It was an inspired plan. The crowd was so fixated on the mime that they didn't notice the little band of dancers who set up their boom box at the edge of the circle. When Benny raised his paw, Woody pressed the play button.

The five imitated the walk of the mime, who by that time was imitating the toddle of a baby clinging to his

82

mother's finger. Then the Rattoons swiveled, snapped their hats, and moved forward in a single line into one of their favorite routines to the tune of "Royal Rat Blues."

"Five, six, seven, eight, walk, right, left, right, left, five, six, seven, eight, pivot, five, six, brush, eight, pas de bourrée, arm up . . ." Under her breath, Ella was talking them through the steps, but none of them needed it because they were dancing their hearts out, moving as if they were one.

The audience was stunned into complete silence. In the back, people were jumping up and down trying to see what everybody was watching. In the front row, some people began to tap their feet to the music. The mime turned around, affected the position of a stunned onlooker, and held it. For once, he didn't seem to be playing a part.

Then high above the crowd, a little boy cried, "Mommy, look, the mice are dancing."

"Those aren't mice, son," said a deep voice somewhere in the back. "They're rats."

14

ARRE*S*TED

The reaction was immediate and vio-
lent. The crowd began to back away.
People screamed and crashed into one
another in their hurry to escape. Several
sprinted for the taxi stand. Two fought each other to
get into a moving cab, while a third scrambled onto the
roof and clung to the neon sign advertising a Broadway
show.

"Run for it," Benny said when he saw a guard headed
their way, followed by two men with huge brooms. With
the boom box banging against Woody's legs, they sprinted
down the avenue. Monk had been right. There was a park, a
great big one with trees and bushes and a million places to
hide. They scampered past a line of artists selling their
wares on the sidewalk and crossed two driveways, right
between the wheels of a waiting truck.

Bang, a broom landed on their right and they skittered
left. An umbrella narrowly missed Ella's ear. One car
screeched to a halt on the avenue and another rammed into
its trunk. The two drivers jumped out and began to yell at

each other. Somebody threw a hat at the rats. It landed right on top of Woody, but he slid out from underneath without missing a stride.

"Into the park," Benny called, and like a cavalry commander leading a charge, he pointed right with his cane raised high. They took the corner on one paw and followed Benny into a particularly dense line of bushes along the wall.

"Bloody vermin," shouted a voice. "We'll get you." The broom wielders had been joined by a policeman and an old lady with a small yappy dog.

"Napoleon will find them," she cried.

"Don't let that dog off the leash, lady," said the policeman. "It's against the rules."

"Officer, don't be a nincompoop. My dog is a Jack Russell. They are specifically trained to catch rats. Nappy will snap them up in a minute."

"Listen, lady, we'll take care of this business. You and your dog move along now."

During this argument, the five Rattoons had been scurrying away along the wall. The voices grew fainter.

"That dog ought to be called Yappy," muttered Woody.

"Or Snappy," said Fletcher.

"The bartender at the Goat told me about Jack Russells," Ella said, her eyes wide. "He said they're the best dogs in the world for catching rats."

"So let's not give him the chance," Monk gasped. "Keep going, Benny."

Benny had no intention of stopping. The underbrush thickened, and they hugged a stone wall that ran right next to a major highway of some sort. The deafening roar of the passing cars normally would have stopped the rats in their tracks, but the threat of that dog's teeth sunk deep into their flesh was enough to keep them moving along at a brisk clip. Finally Benny called a halt, and they leaned against the wall to catch their breath.

"I think they've given up," he said.

The rest of them nodded. They were leaning over, gasping. Nobody looked at Benny. Nobody said anything for a long while.

Fletcher was the first to speak. "Well, that was a disaster," he said.

"Our dancing was great," Ella ventured in a timid voice. "Timing was perfect, the combinations fluid."

"Switchtail was right," Monk said. "It's too dangerous up here with the humans."

"Those Acrobrats were sneaky creeps," Woody said. "Telling us we should come up here. They must have known what was going to happen. They were just trying to get rid of us for good."

But Benny knew what they weren't saying. They weren't saying that he had gotten them into this terrible mess and how could they ever trust him to get them out of it.

Fletcher handed out their tap shoes, which would hold up better on the rough terrain.

Suddenly Monk put his nose to the air. "I smell rats," he said in a low voice. "Coming this way. From the west."

The five pressed their backs against the wall and waited. In the distance, they heard a small ratlike voice that gradually grew louder as it approached. "Count off." Then a series of different voices that sang out, "One, two, three, four, five, six." The leader again: "Column right, march." The tramp of paws changed direction and moved closer. "Left, right, left, right. Count off." The one voice was joined by a chorus of others singing in 3/4 marching time.

They swung into sight, a smart little band of marching rats, three rows, two abreast, dressed in gray uniforms that blended with the color of their fur. Long-handled wire brushes rested on their shoulders, and they carried these with obvious pride. Two in the rear had plastic forks stuck like knives through their belts. The squad was led by a smaller rat, brandishing what looked like a scoop.

"Halt," cried the leader, his scoop raised to the sky. "Right flank, march. Left flank, march." Before they knew it, the Rattoons were surrounded, the wire brushes barely inches from their snouts.

"These are the ones, sir," offered a soldier, sighting Monk down the barrel of his brush.

"How can you be sure?"

"The report said five of them. And look at the way they're dressed. Not your normal street clothes, exactly."

"I believe you're right, Sergeant. Take them into custody. We will await orders from HQ."

"Run," Benny cried, but it was too late. The circle closed around them. Paws gripped their wrists. The boom box was ripped from Woody's grasp and his right arm twisted up behind his back.

"No use struggling," the sergeant said calmly.

It didn't take them any time at all to realize how hopeless their situation was. Without further ado, the Rattoons were handcuffed together, with a fancy silver chain that some human had once worn around her neck, and marched off in double time.

Evening had fallen, and the park was emptying of people. When they crossed a wooden bridge, the rush of cars passing so far below made Fletcher dizzy, and he began to sway in the line.

"You all right, Fletch?" Woody whispered.

"Silence among the prisoners," said the leader.

Ella counted each step they took to distract herself from their desperate predicament. At first, Monk tried to keep track of where they were going so he could lead them out again if the chance ever came. But they switched directions so often that he became hopelessly turned around and finally gave up.

Benny trudged along, his shoulders in a slump. Another wrong decision, he thought. He had been sure that fellow rats would treat them better than those humans, but it didn't look that way. These soldiers or whatever they were had refused to answer any questions, and whenever one of the Rattoons slowed down, he was poked in the backside with the sharp tines of a plastic fork. They had been subjected to a humiliating search. The boom box and Fletcher's costume suitcase had been confiscated along with Monk's maps.

None of them knew their destination or how long this forced march would continue.

15

THE DESIGNATED FORAGERS

At long last, the squad leader raised his paw and called halt. The prisoners were blindfolded and forced down on all fours. Branches snapped in their faces, and nasty thorns caught in their tails.

Finally they stumbled out into some kind of clearing and the leader's voice said, "The prisoners, Lieutenant."

A deep female voice said, "Inspection arms. Port arms. At ease."

All around them, the Rattoons could feel the shift in their guards' movements, the rattle of brush handles smacking the ground.

"You may remove the blindfolds," said the female. "Do not release them."

"Yes, ma'am," said the squad leader. He barked a command at the squad.

The five stood blinking uncertainly in the bright light of a campfire. They had been brought into some kind of headquarters where a number of tents were set up in a circle. From one of them, the smell of melting cheese rose and wafted through the air. Monk almost fainted from hunger. He could barely remember the morning pancake.

Still chained together, the Rattoons sank in unison to the ground and watched as rats glided swiftly about the little encampment, cleaning their weapons, preparing for dinner, stoking the fire. In front of one of the tents, the lieutenant, a gaunt gray rat with long limbs, sat making notes at a table. From time to time, she glanced their way, but she said nothing to them.

"What's going to happen to us?" Ella whispered.

The others shrugged.

"I hope they feed us before they call in the firing squad," Monk muttered.

"Always your stomach first," Fletcher said, but his complaint was halfhearted. He was hungry, too, he had to admit, and the smells issuing from the mess tent were tantalizing.

"Who are they?" Ella asked.

"Good question," remarked the lieutenant, who had crossed the clearing noiselessly to stand above them. Ella jumped at the sharp bark of her voice. "The 117th Battalion of the DFs, Museum Squad."

"Designated Foragers," Ella said in an awed whisper.

"Shadrach told us about you," Monk said brightly, but subsided into silence at a withering look from the lieutenant.

"Whoever Mr. Shadrach is, there is obviously a great deal that he didn't tell you. From what I understand, you have no passports, visas, or transmittal papers of any kind. Am I correct?"

"Yes, sir," said Benny. "I mean, ma'am."

She looked at him over the paper she was holding. "Don't act smart with me."

"I'm not, sir. Ma'am."

"Therefore you have not been given official permission to travel aboveground. Am I correct?"

"We didn't know we needed permission," Benny said.

"Just answer my question. Yes or no."

"No, ma'am, no permission."

"That means you are in violation of code number 4723. Tomorrow you shall be escorted to the tribunal to stand trial. Any witnesses you can call for your defense will be contacted when we hand you over to the custody of the Hollow Police. I should warn you that violations of this code are taken very seriously, and I for one shall recommend you get the most severe punishment allowable by law. Would you like to know why?"

Benny opened his mouth, but no sound came out.

"Yes," Fletcher squeaked at last. "We didn't mean to do anything wrong."

"I am not in the slightest bit interested in what you meant or did not mean to do." The rat drew herself to her full height. "Rodents like yourselves must stand trial for their actions, not their foolish intentions. Because of the pandemonium you caused this afternoon in front of the museum, the humans will raise a hue and cry. Tomorrow their papers will be filled with this story. The city council will issue new laws; the mayor will appear on television calling for the eradication of our entire species. More traps will be laid, more poisons spread. By your actions, you have endangered the life of every rat who works aboveground. Have I made myself perfectly clear?"

The five miserable rats nodded.

She pulled out her pencil and gave it a lick. "I must make a full report. Which one of you will be answering my questions?"

Benny raised a paw, and the chain wrapped tightly around his skinny wrist clinked up and down the line.

"Name?"

"Benny Hornblower Rattoon."

"Age?"

"Fifteen rat years."

She went on barking questions and Benny went on answering in a solemn monotone until suddenly her voice softened. "Your father's name was Art. Arthur what?"

"Nobody ever called him Arthur, ma'am. He was Art Hornblower."

"And your mother's name was Sally, correct?"

Benny nodded. He hadn't even mentioned his mother.

"Sally Scat Rat," she said before he could speak again.

"You knew them?" Ella asked. For once, the lieutenant didn't snap at her for speaking out of turn.

"I certainly did," she said, and her eyes seemed to be watching something in the distance. "On our first date my mate took me to the Boom Boom Room. Your mother sang 'A Fine Rat Romance,' and we went back every Saturday night after that. When Harold proposed to me, they brought us up onstage and your father played that horn. Your mother sang 'The Rat I Love,' and we danced until the sun came up. Oh, did we dance." She stopped speaking. Not one of them moved. The rats gliding around the camp looked up from their chores at the sudden silence. By the light of the fire, Benny saw the glint of a tear as it slid down her cheek.

"Did you marry him?"

"I did. So many glorious years together until—" She stopped again, and this time her body trembled from head to tail. "Enough of this," she snapped, her voice tense. "Your height."

"Ten inches, not counting my tail."

"Weight?"

Benny went on answering the questions.

"Your purpose in coming aboveground? I have to ask this question although I find it ridiculous. If you are not a DF or a licensed scavenger, you have no purpose being aboveground at all."

"To dance," said Benny.

"To what?" she asked.

"To dance. We're a tap and jazz group called the Rat-toons. We were told the best place to attract an audience was on the front steps of the museum. The Acrobrats told us to come here."

"Oh yes, I remember them. They were responsible for the last great purge. Swinging along some wire they'd attached to a lamppost. And some human below calling out encouragement."

"That must have been Oliver String Bean Bailey," Ella whispered to Woody.

"What did the tribunal give them? What punishment?" Monk asked.

"The usual, I believe. They were forced to hang by their tails for ten days above a vat of boiling oil."

"But that's no punishment for a ship rat. They hang by their tails just to eat their dinner," Woody said. "I knew those Acrobrats had it in for us. I remember the way they looked at each other when they told us how to get aboveground."

"Well, you should have thought of that before you attempted this ridiculous exercise." But once again her voice seemed to soften. "Dancing, you say."

The squad leader appeared beside her. "Your dinner is ready, ma'am."

"I'll be there in a minute," she said. "Have you got something for them?"

"The guards are preparing to feed them."

Monk's stomach growled in anticipation, and she glanced in his direction. "Sounds as if it's not a moment too soon for you. What's your name?"

"Monk," he said. "We could dance for you."

"This is a military base, young rat, not a speakeasy." But her voice wavered.

"It would be a show for the troops," Fletcher said quickly. "I bet they need entertainment after so many hard hours in the field."

"The soldiers are a bit restless, ma'am," muttered the squad leader. "They were very disturbed to learn that all leaves have been canceled."

"Well, they can thank this pack of dancers for that."

"Exactly," Benny said. "It will be our way of trying to make it up to them."

She stared at him for a long time. "And next you'll tell me that you can't dance in chains."

"I'm afraid so. But I promise we won't try to escape."

"Are you a rat to be trusted?"

"I'm Art and Sally's oldest son. You trusted them, didn't you?"

"What's he talking about?" asked the squad leader.

She turned away. "After dinner, then," was all she said before retiring to her tent.

16

DANCING IN THE DARK

 "What good will this do?" Woody whispered to Benny once she'd left. Benny shrugged. "It was Monk's idea. Ask him."

"She might let us go," Monk said.

"No way," said Woody, but their spirits lifted a little. Who knew what she would do? After all, she'd known Ma and Pa. She'd danced with her mate to their music. And if they were to be delivered to the tribunal tomorrow, what better way to spend their last night than dancing?

Ella and Woody conferred on the music and chose to start with their mother's rendition of "Fur Flies." If anything was to soften the lieutenant's resolve, it would be Sally's pure, clean voice rising from the boom box to the sky above the dark trees. Just when Monk was sure they had forgotten all about feeding the prisoners, a guard named Jerry rolled over a cart with five bowls of garbage stew. The smell was delicious and they dug in, snouts first.

"Monk," Woody snapped. "Remember your manners." But Monk couldn't hear a thing over the noise of his slurping.

The guard stood and watched them eat. "Don't imagine you'll do much dancing with full bellies," he snorted.

"Tell me something," Benny said in a low voice. "What happened to the lieutenant's mate?"

The guard looked over his shoulder and then leaned closer. "We're not supposed to talk about him. He was poisoned last year. Fish bait mixed with anticoagulants. Oldest trick in the book, but he fell for it. She kept trying to make the old guy retire, but he said he wouldn't know what to do with himself if he weren't out in the field."

"Are they done yet?" called a voice, and Jerry snapped to attention.

"Not quite, sir. In a moment."

He leaned over again and whispered the rest of his story in a rush. "For a long time, the same old human from Rodent Control was putting out the bait, and we never took anything of his. We called him Frenchie. The bait was always old and moldy, and it stank of his cologne. We knew not to touch that stuff. But the day after that high-wire show, some young guy took over, and that one knew how to bait. We're pretty sure he got old Harold, I mean the sergeant, his first day on the job." He jerked his snout over his shoulder. "Vera ain't been the same since. Control's been trying to get her to retire, but she won't go in. Maybe she thinks she's going to meet up with Harold out there somewhere. Getting a little dotty herself, if you ask me." He straightened up. "All right, pass those bowls forward. Enough slopping around, you prisoners," he ordered. They understood that the sharp voice he was using was meant to impress his superiors.

"What's an anticoag-whatever?" Ella whispered as he was stacking the bowls.

"You bleed to death, sister. It's one nasty way to go." And without another word, he melted into the darkness on the other side of the campfire.

○　●　○　●　○

After supper, the lieutenant set up her chair in front of her tent and the rat soldiers settled themselves on the ground around her.

"Hope you're ready," muttered the squad leader. "We don't have all night, you know."

"Yes, sir," Benny said. He gave Woody the signal, the opening notes blew out of Art's horn, and their feet began to shuffle to their mother's joyous voice. "Nothing but fur flying from now on," she sang, and they closed their eyes and tried to make their limbs dance to the music as if they believed the words.

It didn't work. What had they been thinking? The tap shoes made no noise at all in the soft dirt of the park. With no smack of toe against wood to guide them, they fell out of step and stopped in confusion.

The squad leader got to his feet and pressed the stop button on the boom box. "They're fakes," he announced.

"We need to change into our jazz shoes," Woody cried.

"Give us another chance. We forgot about the surface. We need a hard surface."

All eyes swung to the lieutenant, but she seemed to be in some kind of strange trance and sat rooted to her chair. A few of the soldiers called them names, and the others went back to their tents in disgust. When the lieutenant did not move or speak, the squad leader assumed control. Clearly he had been forced to take over for her on other occasions.

"Back in the chains with them," he ordered. "It was a foolish idea to begin with. The music will attract attention."

"Sir," Ella cried. "Please give us another chance."

But it was no use. In a short time, they had been tied back together and left in a miserable line to toss and turn on the cold ground. The squad leader posted lookouts and settled the camp for the night.

"The detail to take the prisoners to the Hollow Police will leave at dawn," they heard him tell one soldier. The guard gave him a snappy salute in reply.

Then all was silent.

17

THE LONG NIGHT

"I don't think I'll be able to hang by my tail for ten days," Monk whispered, close to tears. "I'm still little. My tail isn't even fully grown."

None of them could think of a single comforting word to offer. The fire had been kicked out before the camp retired, and the night felt close and dark. The city seemed a million miles away.

An owl hooted in the distance. Benny rolled closer to Woody. He didn't know that owls lived in the city, but he knew they hunted at night. He remembered the time a sinister shadow had swooped down just above his family as they ran through the fields of corn stubble between the Blue Goat and the barnyard after a late performance. So many rats in one line must have confused the bird, because it sailed away again without diving. But the terror on his father's face showed Benny how close they had come to losing someone.

He heard the slow, steady breathing of his siblings.

They had somehow managed to fall asleep. He wondered how they would ever be able to sleep hanging upside down from their tails. He supposed after enough hours, your body just gave up. But then didn't your tail unfurl? Didn't you drop like a stone into the boiling oil? And wouldn't that be a particularly grisly way to die?

He closed his eyes and thought of the barnyard—the air dusty with grain, the cozy nests they'd made from the hay, the comforting murmur of voices above when the horse and the mule got into some late-night discussion about local county politics. He would give anything in the world to be back there now.

He knew that if he ever got them out of this mess, they were going to take the train directly back to the barnyard. His mother had made his father leave the city because she thought it was no place to raise a family of rats. Well, she was right about that.

"Wake up, you," a voice whispered urgently. A rat was standing in the shadow of a bush a few feet away. It was the lieutenant. Her gray uniform camouflaged her well except when the moonlight glinted off her incisor teeth. "I've ordered the patrols to stand guard on the other side of the camp," she said. "Wake the rest of the troupe, get your things together, and meet me down that path. Under the lamppost."

"What about the chains?" he asked.

She unwound the knot that bound his wrists together. "You do the rest. Hurry. There's not much time."

The four woke with a start.

"What does she want?" Ella asked.

"She didn't give me time to ask," Benny said as he undid the last of the knots.

They found her waiting under the lamppost as promised, but she shook her head for silence and signaled them to follow. She was carrying the boom box, and it banged every so often against her legs when she shifted it from one paw to the other.

"I could carry that in my backpack," Woody said, itching to get his paws on it again.

She didn't even bother to answer him.

○　　●　　○　　●　　○

She knew the park well and led them through a maze of overgrown paths. The autumn air was crisp, and the rats moved along at a swift pace. Benny wondered what would happen when the camp patrol found them gone. Would they send out search parties, or was this some devious plan the lieutenant had worked out with the squad leader? Lull those stupid barnyard rats into thinking they were facing the tribunal and then lead them to some even darker and more hideous punishment?

They skirted a large body of water, passed a fountain, scuttled up a wide set of stairs, and crossed a road. At one point, the lieutenant shoved them under a park bench, and they huddled together while she watched through the slats for something to pass.

"Migrating hawk," she muttered. "Red-tailed. They love rats."

Monk squeaked in fear.

"Especially the small ones," she said with a glance his way.

"They nested near the barn in the spring," Woody said.

"Here in the city, Rodent Control stops the rat baiting in the spring while the hawks are feeding their chicks. Humans are pretty dumb, but they've figured out one thing. You poison one animal, you poison every animal that eats that animal."

"Oh, great," Fletcher said. "We should be happy because for a few weeks in the spring the humans aren't poisoning us and only the hawks are hunting us."

"Guess humans like hawks better than rats," Ella said miserably.

"Welcome to life aboveground," the lieutenant muttered between clenched teeth.

They got the message.

The six of them ventured out again, pressed even closer together. At least she wasn't bringing them into this wilderness to be used as bird bait, Benny thought.

18

SHOE MUSIC

At last she put up a paw and they stopped, bumping into one another in the confusion.

"Up there," she said, pointing to a huge stage looming above them. "I want you to dance up there."

The Rattoons stared at one another. That guard Jerry had been right. She was a little dotty.

"What are you waiting for?" she said. "You wanted a stage. I got you one."

"Yes, ma'am," said Benny, and he led the troupe up the stairs on the right. As soon as they hit the boards, Monk did a little ball-change, shuffle, and a hop. The slap of his toes against the wooden floor echoed up into the dark branches above them.

"Perfect," he said.

The lieutenant had come up on the stage herself to get a better view. She plunked down the boom box, rewound the tape, and pressed the play button, then folded her limbs and stood at ease. "So dance," she ordered.

And they obeyed the order.

For the first time, they were dancing on a real stage, not the rough wooden planking of a barn floor. The difference was astounding. Never had their taps sounded so clean and crisp. It was as if their feet took on a new life, a rhythm all their own, and in some strange way it seemed as if the dance was dancing them. Their bodies heard the beat, picked it up from their feet, and simply followed along. Ella felt her limbs loosen. Woody raised his paws in the air and clapped them together above his head. Even Benny forgot all that had brought them to this place and all that lay ahead. He lived only in this one moment—in this string of notes—and his tap shoes hammered out a greeting to the stage floor and to the lieutenant and the trees and, beyond that, to the stars in the night sky.

The final note of Art's horn floated away, the shoe music ended, and the Rattoons took a dazed bow. From the lone member of the audience two paws came together, and the Rattoons bowed again. She did not stop clapping for a long time. And when at last there was silence in the band shell, she spoke. "You are free to go."

"Are you sure?" Benny asked.

"Yes, I'm sure. You rats were born to dance. I couldn't live with myself if I took that away from you. Even though you were wrong to come aboveground."

"See you," Woody said. He picked up the boom box and scuttled stage right.

"What will happen to you?" Ella asked.

The lieutenant shrugged. She looked suddenly much older. "I'll be demoted, maybe even court-martialed. But my time has come. I know what they say behind my back. 'The old lady Vera's gone around the bend.'" She stared over their heads into the dark curved recesses of the band shell. "Harold and I danced here, you know. Under the stars when everybody else had gone home."

"You guys coming?" Woody called from the wings.

"Shhh," Ella said.

"What's going on? If she says we can go, we'd better hotpaw it out of here."

"He's right," the lieutenant said with a shudder. Whether it was Woody's words or a sudden cold breeze, something seemed to bring her back to reality. "No reason to hang around listening to me reminiscing. I have my memories. It's time you made yours. So where will you go?"

All eyes turned to Benny. An hour ago, before the dance, he would have said, Give me the fastest route back to the train station. But the crisp clap of their tap shoes against the stage floor had changed his mind.

"We need to get to the Boom Boom Room," he said. "Just to see it once. To say we've been there."

She nodded. Monk pulled out his maps. "You'll have to make your way down through the park to the Children's Zoo," she explained, tracing the route with a thin paw. "That's the nearest tail opener. I haven't used it since they rebuilt the zoo, but I'm told it's a small hole in a fake log." She showed Monk the location of the red dot that marked the zoo. "If you have any trouble finding it, check in with Chilly. He's one of the two potbellied pigs. His mate, Lily, can get grumpy, but he's always willing to share a little food and give free advice. On your way south, stay out of any open fields."

"Because of the red-tailed hawks?" Monk asked.

"And the sharp-shinned and the rough-legged, the golden eagle and the peregrine falcon. Not to mention the owls."

Benny shivered. "We get the idea."

"So, with a little luck, we find the tail opener. Then what?" Fletcher asked.

"You take the Red Line back to the Central Depot and switch to the Blue. Get off at the stop marked Rat Hollow Opera. You'll see the signs to the Boom Boom Room as soon as you leave the train."

"Thanks," Benny said.

"One more thing." She took a piece of paper from her belt pack, scribbled something on it, and handed it to him. "That's a temporary transmittal order. The zoo has a pretty fierce DF battalion. If you run into them, show them this. I've signed it." She looked sternly up and down the row. "No more messing around aboveground, you hear me? Our job up here is tough enough. You do your dancing, but you do it in the Hollow. You won't get a second chance, not from me or anybody else."

They nodded solemnly, and before they could say another word, she had glided down the stage steps and disappeared into the darkness. The five of them stood looking after her. They were alone again.

19

THE ZOO

They scuttled along, their bodies low to the ground, moving stealthily from one overhanging bush to the next. Monk kept them as close to the park wall as possible, although from time to time, they were forced to move out into the open.

At one point, as they caught their breath under a park bench, Ella nudged Fletcher in the side.

"They may not put our paintings in the museum, but look at that. Somebody's drawn a picture of us and stuck it out here for all the world to see. That should make you happy." She pointed at a black-and-white poster of a rat with oversize ears and an extra-long tail. "But why is there a red line running right through the middle of its belly?"

"Pretty terrible artist, if you ask me," Fletcher said. He took a moment to check the sky for hawks and then scooted out to peer more closely at Ella's discovery. He came back, shaking his head.

"That's not art, Ella," he said. "It's a warning. Rat poison all around here."

Monk lifted his head from a puddle of sticky brown liquid that had spilled out of a red plastic cup. "Could this be poisoned?" he asked, his tongue still hanging out.

"Anything could," Benny said.

Monk froze. For a moment, nothing moved except his tongue, which rolled smoothly and silently back into his mouth.

○   •   ○   •   ○

They made their way up the short slope to the Children's Zoo and ducked under the turnstile.

"Left or right?" Woody asked.

"Don't think it matters," Monk said, consulting his map one more time.

They stood for a moment on a small bridge, their noses lifted to an assortment of smells, some oddly familiar and others foreign.

"I smell food," Monk said. No call to arms brought a regiment faster into line than that announcement from their youngest brother.

"Lead on, O special snout," Fletcher said, and the rest fell over themselves to follow Monk. They ducked under the bushes. Birds they had never seen before stirred and twittered in the lower branches.

"What are you?" Ella whispered to a squat bird with enormous red feet.

The bird opened one eye. "A chukar," he said. "What are you?"

"Norway rat."

"Common brown," the odd bird said.

Ella stuck out her tongue at him, but the chukar had already closed his eye again.

"There's a net above us," Fletcher said, staring up through the leaves. "Must be to keep the birds in."

"That's the idea," said a dove with a crested peak. "The place looks good to the tourists, but it's nothing but one great big cage."

"Birdseed," called Monk from the front of the line. "That's what I smelled."

"Mind if we help ourselves?" Benny asked. "We've been on the road most of the night."

"Eat away," replied the dove. "The keepers refill it twice a day."

The five gathered around the low bowl and ate their fill. It had been a long night, and Jerry's garbage stew was nothing but a distant memory. In no time at all, the container was empty and Monk had hopped right into the bowl and was chasing the last bit of seed with his tongue. Benny dragged him out by his tail.

"Looks like he was ready to start chewing the plastic," remarked a lop-eared rabbit from his side of a wire fence.

"Excuse me, sir, could you tell me where we might find a tail opener?" Fletcher asked.

"No idea what you're talking about," said the rabbit. He flipped an ear over his shoulder and called out, "Dutchy, wake up a minute. Ever hear of something called a tail opener?"

The reply was inaudible.

"It's inside a fake log," Woody said hopefully.

"Take a look around, rat. Practically every log in this place is made of plastic. Not to mention the trees, the bridge you just crossed, and those ridiculous-looking fake rabbits." He waved one ear at a cluster of vague forms in the corner. "Humans seem to think fake wood looks better than real wood."

"Do you happen to know some pigs called Chilly and Lily?" Benny asked.

"Never met them, mind you," said the rabbit. "But they live just on the other side of the zoo. You can go out the entrance and back in through the exit. Their pen is next to the rest rooms." The rabbit snorted. "Kind of appropriate, wouldn't you say? Anyway, I wouldn't wake them too early. They're a little out of sorts right now."

"Why?" Ella asked.

"Heard the keepers talking about putting them on a diet. But it may be nothing. Rumors spread like wildfire in this place."

20

CHILLY AND LILY

 The sky was lightening in the east as the rats made their way down the short slope and up the other side.

"The humans are going to start coming in here soon," Benny said. "We've got to find this tail opener and be on our way."

Woody yawned. "A little nap wouldn't be a bad thing either. This backpack is getting heavy."

"Here's the pigpen," Monk called.

The five rats peered through the fence. In the pale dawn light, they could make out a green plastic swimming pool filled with mud in the middle of the pen and beyond that a water bowl. Two large dark lumps lay in the hay under a shed in the corner.

"Mr. Chilly," Benny called softly. "Excuse me, could you give us a moment?" Nothing stirred.

Fletcher picked up a pawful of gravel and hurled it at the side of the shed. The shower of small rocks made a sudden rattle in the stillness. In a neighboring pen, the goats stirred.

"What's that?" bleated one.

"Go back to sleep, Onyx," muttered another. "It's not time for breakfast yet."

"That didn't work," said Woody.

"Yes, it did," said Ella. "One of them's moving."

An enormous pig struggled to its feet and waddled out to the fence. Its black leathery skin was covered all over with a pelt of wispy hair, and its long tail waved back and forth like a dog's. It peered at the rats from under a rolling shelf of eyebrows.

"Are you Mr. Chilly?" asked Ella.

The pig snorted. "He never was a mister, never will be. He's Chilly. I'm Lily. Did you bring us some food?"

"Well, no," said Benny. "Somebody told us you'd know where the tail opener is."

Her eyes narrowed until they almost disappeared in the folds of fat. "Well, maybe I do, and then again, maybe I don't. It depends on what you're willing to pay for the information."

"Pay?" asked Fletcher in an outraged voice. "Listen, Miss Lily, we're kind of in trouble here. Now, why don't you try to help out a group of visitors who need some directions?"

"Rat, in this town, you don't get nothing for nothing. Sooner you learn that, the better," said the pig.

"Wait," cried Benny. "What kind of food do you want?"

"Fruit," she said, and her enormous damp snout began to move back and forth in anticipation. It reminded Monk of the slimy foot of a snail. "Try that garbage can over there. The cleaning people were in a terrible hurry to get home last night and they didn't empty that one. I was watching."

"I just bet you were," said Fletcher under his breath. "I bet you don't miss a trick."

"Stupid keepers have taken us off fruit," Lily said. "Something about sugar making us fat. Look at us," she roared. "We're potbellied pigs. Aren't we supposed to be round?"

They took a step back and eyed her. Her large belly swung back and forth, scraping the ground as she moved, and rolls of lard slid down off her pointy ears like grilled cheese oozing out of a sandwich.

"That fat?" Ella whispered.

"Who asked your opinion, rodent?" said Lily. "Just get me some fruit and you'll be on your way."

Monk was sent off to scout the garbage can while the rest stood at a respectful distance and waited.

"Lily, what's going on?" asked the other pig as he shambled up to the fence and peered at the rats.

"Pipe down, old man, I'm getting us some fruit."

"But we're not supposed to eat sugar anymore," said Chilly.

"Miss Priss," she spat.

"Good morning, Mr. Chilly," said Benny. "We are the Rattoons, a group of jazz and tap rats making our way back to Rat Hollow, and we were wondering—"

"Don't tell him a thing," said Lily, glaring alternately at the rats and her partner. Chilly took a step to the side. Clearly he'd already experienced the full extent of her wrath on many a previous occasion and was staying clear this time. He was shorter than Lily, smaller in girth, and nimbler on his feet.

"Jazz and tap?" he said to Benny politely, but before Benny could draw breath to speak again, there came a terrible commotion from the nearest garbage can. Monk backed out, his teeth buried deep into one side of a grapefruit rind, while another rat hung on just as fiercely to the other.

"Grapefruit," Lily cried in glee. "My absolute favorite."

By this time, the two rats were rolling over and over in the dirt and the grapefruit skin was looking much the worse for wear. Monk's siblings rushed to his rescue, and when the stranger rat saw the reinforcements, he opened his mouth and backed away.

"You must be a DF," Benny said, eyeing the gray uniform.

"What are you all doing aboveground?" asked the rat as he straightened his jacket and dusted off his buttons.

"Special pass," said Benny, and he whipped out the piece of paper from the lieutenant. "We're trying to find the nearest tail opener."

"The grapefruit," Lily snorted, her snout shoved through the wires of her pen. "Just pass me the grapefruit, you nice little rat."

"I wasn't such a nice rat a minute ago," Monk replied. He gave the grapefruit a couple of licks and beamed. "Yummy, yummy," he said.

Lily beat her head against the fence post and groaned.

"Lily, you're on a diet," said the DF. "Just wait a few hours and you'll have a nourishing breakfast of zucchini and carrots."

"All very well for you to say," said Lily. "Why don't you try surviving on that rabbit food?"

"Now, now, my little raspberry," said Chilly in a comforting voice. "We're really very lucky, you know, not having to forage for ourselves out there in the great world."

"Oh, do be quiet, you old beet green."

The DF rolled his eyes. He'd obviously heard more of these discussions than he had the patience for. He motioned to the rats to follow him down the path.

"What shall I do with the grapefruit?" Monk asked.

The DF turned it over a couple of times with his snout. "Oh, give it to her. Don't think the Ratomat inspectors would accept it in that condition anyway."

Lily fell on the grapefruit with a cry of joy and swallowed the thick yellow rind in two bites.

"She didn't even say thank you," Monk said.

"No wonder Chilly's so much thinner," said Ella.

"That's all they get to eat? Zucchini and carrots?" asked Woody.

The DF nodded toward a couple of machines standing by the goat pen. "The humans put quarters in those slots and buy pellets to feed to the animals. But most of the time they feed the goats. Not too many people want Lily's great slimy snout touching their skin. Sometimes I actually feel kind of sorry for her. Last week I heard a woman say, 'Ooh, aren't they nasty hogs. Don't get near them, you children.' Comments like that day in and day out could turn any animal sour."

He brought them to a halt next to a log covered with enormous fake turtle shells.

"What are those for?" Ella asked.

"Human children stick their bodies inside and pretend to be turtles. Their parents wave and squeal. Seems to be some form of human ritual." He gave Benny back the transmittal papers. "How's the lieutenant doing? I hear things have been rough since the sergeant was taken."

The Rattoons looked at one another. "She's doing okay," Fletcher offered. "She's a tough old rat."

"Best in the division," the DF said. "Well, good luck. You'll find the tail opener halfway down the length of this log. Sorry I can't hang around any longer or I'll be late for my divisional rendezvous."

"Thanks a lot," Benny said as the rat trotted off.

21

LAYOVER

"Ready?" Benny said as they took one last look around the zoo.

"No," said Woody. His snout was in the air. "I smell home."

"What are you talking about?" Fletcher asked. They all raised their noses and breathed in deeply. Before anybody else could speak, Woody had trotted off down the path, following a wonderfully familiar smell of hay and grain dust and manure.

"Woody," Benny cried. "Come back. We've got to get out of here."

"Follow him," Monk said, and they chased along behind with Benny bringing up the rear. They hopscotched over a set of metal lily pads, dashed under the swinging plastic tapes that hung over the hole in an enormous fake tree, and scampered down a path of soft mulch.

They screeched to a halt in the middle of a circle of pens where a number of curious goats, sheep, one cow, and a long, leggy, bushy-faced horse hung their heads over the fence to stare at them. Pictures of these same animals were posted in the corners. A quick scan of the information signs revealed that their audience included a few pygmy goats, a number of sheep with foreign-sounding names such as Tunis and Cotswold and St. Croix, a Dexter cow, and one alpaca.

"So you're not a horse," Monk said out of the blue.

The bushy head tilted to the side. "I most certainly am not. Never have been, never will be."

"Have you seen our brother?" Benny asked before this group could distract them.

"He went thataway," said one of the sheep with a toss of his head. "Right into the middle of our hay pile."

"And I'm not coming out," Woody cried from inside the pen.

"Come on, Woody," Benny called back. "We don't have time for this kind of nonsense. We only have a few minutes to get back to the Hollow."

"We need rest," Woody declared. "And this is the closest thing to home we'll ever find. Come on in. Wait till you feel how soft this nest is."

In the distance, they heard the clang of a bucket.

"Keepers," said another sheep. "Breakfast time."

"They're not too partial to rats," murmured Dexter, the black cow. "'Spect you all better take cover."

The four trotted nimbly between the four feet of the alpaca and dove for cover under the hay. It smelled sweet and dusty and cheerful.

"Mmm," said Ella, burrowing deep into the pile. "It's so warm."

Nobody else spoke. They rolled up close, curled their tails, and drifted off to sleep without another word.

○   •   ○   •   ○

Fletcher woke to the sound of chewing. He opened his eyes and found himself a mere two inches from the rough tongue of the alpaca. "Watch out," he squeaked.

"Not to worry," said the alpaca. "I don't eat meat. You had a nice nap. It's close to suppertime."

Fletcher peered out. The dull, gray sky looked threatening.

"Weather coming," said the alpaca. "About time. I could use some cooling down."

The others were still asleep, and Fletcher decided not to wake them.

"What's there to see around here?"

"Lot of humans, usually. Not today, though. Colder the weather, the fewer visitors we get."

"Besides humans. Any museums?"

"Not that I know of. There is a clock tower over by the other part of the zoo. Some days, when the wind's blowing in the right direction, we can hear the bells. They ring on the half hour. Some famous sculptor made it. They tell us it has lots of different animals carrying instruments."

"What animals?" Fletcher asked eagerly.

The alpaca tossed his head. The bushy bangs flopped up and down, and for one brief moment, Fletcher saw his eyes.

"How would I know what animals? I haven't seen anything but the inside of this pen since I was four months old."

"There's another part of the zoo?" Fletcher asked.

"Yup. Down the path and under a little bridge, from what the pigeons tell us. They have a seal pond and polar bears, some penguins. Summertime, people come to us; winter, they're over there. Standing in heated rooms looking at ice caps. Hard to figure."

"Think I'll take a look around," Fletcher said. "When the rest wake up, tell them I'll be back before dark."

Not too many humans, and the hawks didn't hunt much during the day, he thought as he slunk out of the pen. Truth be told, he was reluctant to go back to the Hollow without one more look around aboveground.

There was nobody in sight except a small boy who was playing bullfighter with the metal cow near Dexter's pen. He'd smack the cow's button to produce the recorded lowing sound and then taunt the beast with a wave of his paper napkin. Dexter looked amused at the boy's antics, and occasionally, he mooed himself to add some realism to the game.

"Cesar," a human voice called. The boy swatted the cow one more time before he ran off.

Fletcher waited until Cesar had disappeared around the corner before he made his way through the thick undergrowth toward the front entrance.

22

THE HORN-BLOWING RAT

The jangle of keys and low human voices woke the rest of them. They froze in place, staring through the dim, dusty air at one another's terrified eyes.

There was a grunt and the shuffle of human feet. A great shower of hay came down on the rats. Tough as it was to breathe, they stayed where they were.

"Hey, Dexter, old moo face, how you doing?" bellowed a female voice, followed by the slap of a hand on what was probably the cow's rump. "Cold enough for you?"

"Radio was talking about snow," said a male.

"Oh, great. Soon we're going to have to lock these critters in their pens and turn on the heaters." The female keeper cackled. "And phew, the stench when you open up those doors in the morning. That'll be your job. I'm going permanent on the afternoon shift."

Their voices drifted out of hearing.

"You can come out now," said a sheep who was pushing her nose through the hay. "They won't be back. They're finished for the day."

The rats dug their way to the top of the pile and shook themselves. Ella picked three pieces of hay from Monk's shoulders.

"Come on, Fletcher," Benny called. "Time to rise and shine. It's nearly dark."

No answer.

"He's not even talking in his sleep," Woody said.

"Dig down and get him, Monk, will you?" said Benny.

"No use," said the sheep. "Juan told me your brother decided to take a little look around. Said he'd be back before dark."

"Who's Juan?" asked Ella.

"The alpaca," said Monk in a low voice. "The one I thought was a horse."

"A little look around?" said Woody. "Where?"

"When I saw him, he was headed for the front entrance," said Dexter, who had leaned his large black head over the fence. "A while ago. He didn't bother to tell me where he was going."

Benny walked over to a fence post and began beating his head methodically against it. "I give up. I absolutely, positively give up. I refuse to take responsibility for any of you anymore. It's too big a job. I don't know why Switchtail gave it to me."

The goats and sheep gathered around and eyed Benny nervously. The three siblings looked at one another in horror. Their older brother had never behaved this way before.

"Benny, don't do that," Monk cried.

"We're all responsible for ourselves," Woody said in a sharp voice. "Now, pull yourself together. We have to find Fletcher and be on our way."

Ella walked up and gave Benny a kick on his backside.

They weren't sure which method worked, but Benny stopped. He rubbed his forehead and looked slightly embarrassed.

"You all right now?" Monk asked.

Benny nodded and switched to rubbing his backside. "Wish you hadn't been wearing your tap shoes, Ella," he said.

"Sorry about that. Now, think. What are we going to do?"

Benny turned to the assembled animals who had been watching this little family drama with interest. "Any idea where our brother went?"

Juan stepped forward. "To see the clock. He asked about a museum, but I said there weren't any that I knew of. But there's a clock with animals playing instruments."

"Oh no," Ella groaned. "He's looking for art again. The rat's obsessed."

o   •   o   •   o

Fletcher hunkered down under the shelter of a small bridge, waiting for the animals of the Delacorte Clock to take their turn at the half hour. It wasn't safe to get closer because a small group of humans was doing the same thing.

Finally the chimes started and the animals began their circle dance. Each one turned slowly on his own pedestal, playing his instrument. Fletcher stood motionless and studied the animals as they passed. The elephant squeezing the accordion was followed by the hippo on violin, then some kind of bird on drums and a goat blowing his pipes. Animal musicians. And a famous human sculptor had chosen to carve them going around and around the clock, high up for all to see. It was a wonder. And then to Fletcher's utter amazement, a full-sized rat playing a horn turned the corner. He clapped his paws over his mouth. It was as if he had dreamed this great big beautiful rodent, this memorial to his father, right into the sculptor's head. In the dimming afternoon light, the outlines of the bronze animal merged with the brickwork of the clock tower. By the time Fletcher crept closer to get a better look, the magnificent horn-blowing rat had turned the corner and the chimes were done.

Suddenly the humans began to walk directly toward him. He leapt into the middle of a bush. A child must have caught sight of him because there followed an animated discussion and much pointing in his direction before the group finally moved away up the path.

Fletcher stayed in the bush for a long time, trying to decide what to do. It was growing dark, and he knew the others would be awake by now and worried. After peering out to check the sky and the sidewalk, he decided to cross the open space. He had to see that rat one more time before he went back to the Hollow, and he didn't have time to wait for the chimes to sound and the animals to take their turn again.

He scuttled along the line of bushes, made a run for a park bench, and then took shelter in the shadow of the clock tower. A maintenance man emptied a garbage can and dragged the plastic bag away. A hot-dog vendor tipped his cart and rolled it toward the park entrance. A lady strapped her child in a stroller and headed south. Silence. Fletcher glanced left and right. The coast was clear.

He tiptoed out into the middle of the path and looked up. Too close. The clock rat was standing in the shadows. He backed up, stared, backed up some more.

"Hey, watch where you're going," said a voice in his ear. It was a pigeon picking at the last crumbs of a discarded bagel.

"You live around here?" Fletcher asked.

"Here and there. Why?"

"You been up to the top of that clock tower?"

The pigeon shrugged. "Who remembers where I've been?"

"The animal playing the horn. It's a rat, isn't it?"

"Doubt it," said the pigeon, and went back to her strutting and pecking.

"Why do you say that?" Fletcher had shaded his eyes to see if that might help him make out the animal's form.

"Humans don't like rats. Don't like us either. You know what they call us? Rats with wings. Nice, isn't it?"

"Could you do me a quick favor? Just fly up there and see what that animal is. I don't have time to wait for the next turnaround."

"Which animal?" she asked, following the direction of his outstretched paw.

"The one in the corner, playing the horn."

"I'm nearsighted, but I'll take a look. Watch my bagel, will you? Don't let Harvey get it."

"Who's Harvey?"

"The fat pigeon over by the turnstile. He's my brother." With that the pigeon flapped a couple of times and soared to an easy landing next to the clock. She sashayed over to the horn blower, stared up the length of him, and floated back down to Fletcher.

"Bad news, rat. It's a kangaroo."

"What's a kangaroo?"

"Australian animal. Carries its baby in a pocket."

"Are you absolutely sure?" Fletcher asked. He couldn't believe it; he wouldn't. What did a stupid old pigeon know about art?

She lifted her head suddenly as if she could read his thoughts. "I was born near the Bronx Zoo, buddy. I know everything there is to know about species." Her eyes shifted to something over his right shoulder. "Uh-oh, time to skedaddle," and with that remark she took off again just as Fletcher heard someone cry, "Get him, Nappy!"

He turned around to see a small bundle of a dog tearing toward him at top speed with an energetic white-haired human lady trotting along behind, waving her umbrella.

Something about this situation seemed vaguely familiar to Fletcher, but he didn't stop to ask questions. He took off for the bushes as fast as his skinny legs would carry him.

· 23 ·

NAPOLEON

The little fit of despair seemed to have cleared Benny's head. "We'll wait for Fletcher at the end of the tail-opener log," he announced. "He knows where it is, and I'm sure that's where he'll go first."

"If he comes back here, can you tell him where we went?" Ella asked Dexter.

The cow nodded. A piece of hay was hanging out of the side of his mouth.

"By the way, our father knew a fellow named Dexter who played the tenor saxophone," Woody said. "You wouldn't happen to be related, would you?"

"Doubt it," said Dexter. "Far as I know, our family had no musical talent at all."

"Thanks for the sleepover," Woody said to the goats and the sheep.

"Anytime," bleated one of the Tunis.

"Take care of yourselves," called Juan.

With a last wave, they made their way through the undergrowth, crossed back over the little stream, and lined up at the end of the turtle log.

When they were all in place, Benny pricked up his ears. "What is that noise?" he asked in a low voice.

In the distance they could hear a high-pitched yipping and caterwauling that sounded like a dog on the trail of something. It was growing closer.

Then suddenly, Fletcher came tearing across the bridge. His coat was ripped and his face had a look of terror.

"That dog, Nappy," Fletcher cried as he dove into the log.

"Follow Fletcher," Benny said to Woody. "All of you go through the tail opener. I'll hold off the dog here."

Nobody waited to argue. The terrier had become briefly confused by the flapping strands of plastic at the front entrance, but he turned the corner just as Monk disappeared into the log. Benny rose up on his hind legs and bared his teeth.

The sight of a ten-inch rat standing his ground brought the dog to a screeching halt. From the other side of the turnstile, his owner was calling to him. "Napoleon, where are you? Nappy, did you get him, you good little ratter?"

"Nappy," muttered Benny in the fiercest voice he could muster. "I'm one of five. That's four too many for you, I figure."

The dog growled and snapped, enraged at the disappearance of his prey. He had never actually caught a rat, even though his bloodthirsty owner had told him day after day what a good little ratter he was and how noble his ancestral line. Think how she would have crowed with delight if he had broken the back of that strangely dressed rat with one snap of his jaws. Why, right now, he could be trotting back to her with his prize in his teeth.

He'd had that other one on the run, but this one was a different story.

Benny took a step forward. "Go home, Napoleon," he said, keeping the shiver of fear out of his own voice. The dog's teeth looked sharp. Any minute now, he could leap at Benny's throat. But a rat reared up on his hind legs seemed to have given Nappy second thoughts, and Benny was determined to take every advantage of his confusion.

They stood for a long moment, eyeball to eyeball.

"HOME, NAPOLEON!" Benny roared. The dog jumped at the sudden command, turned tail, and ran.

"Well done, rat," clucked the male chukar from under a bush. "Guess you told him what for."

"Guess I did," said Benny. Then he made his way down the log and slipped through the door of the tail opener that Monk was holding open for him.

24

BACK TO THE HOLLOW

Ella took over the costume suitcase while Woody and Benny supported Fletcher between them and Monk carried Woody's backpack. They must have made a strange picture, but down in Rat Hollow, the citizens were polite and asked no questions. On the Red Line, a young bespectacled rat leapt to his feet and offered Fletcher his seat despite the wounded rat's feeble protestations.

They managed to get Fletcher onto the Blue Line and off again at the Rat Hollow Opera stop without incident.

"Look," Ella cried, "there's the sign for the Boom Boom Room."

But food seemed to be more important, so they stopped in at the nearest Ratomat and piled up their trays.

"My, it's good to be back in the Hollow," said Monk once he'd polished off two pizza crusts and half a cheese sandwich. He took in a deep breath. "Good old familiar rat smells whenever you lift your nose."

"How're you doing, Fletch?" Benny asked.

"A little battered. When I stumbled, I could feel his incisors graze my backside."

"You should have seen what Benny did to that dog," Monk said. "He just ordered him to go away and Napoleon turned tail and ran."

All eyes rested on Benny, whose chest filled with pride. He had done that, hadn't he? Stood up and defended his little tribe when the enemy was at the gates.

"You were so brave, Benny," said Ella.

Benny shrugged. "Just did what I had to do. Didn't think about it much, really."

There was a brief silence as they pondered how close a call it had been.

"That little bowlegged owner of his is vicious. She kept egging him on, crying out for my blood." Fletcher shuddered. "What did any rat ever do to her? I thought I was finished. And all for a kangaroo."

"A what?" squeaked Ella.

Fletcher explained. They shook their heads in unison, half in sorrow at Fletcher's disappointment and half in disbelief at his foolishness.

"You gotta give it up, Fletch," said Woody. "This art thing almost cost you your life. And ours. If it hadn't been for Benny, it could have been curtains for all of us."

Fletcher nodded and tried to look solemn and grateful at the same time. They knew this contrite mood of his would never last, but at least they were back down in the Hollow, safe and sound.

"So now what?" Monk asked.

"We agreed we at least wanted to see the Boom Boom Room, right?" Benny said.

Four heads nodded.

"I think we should scout the place and find out if there's any chance of the owners returning soon. If there is, we can wait to do an audition for them. Maybe pick up some odd jobs on the side. After all, this stop is called Rat Hollow Opera. It must be some kind of musical center."

"Sounds like a good plan to me," said Woody as he got to his feet.

"Can someone else help me carry this stuff?" asked Monk.

"Fletcher, you strong enough to walk on your own?" Benny asked.

"Certainly," he said as he hauled himself up. "A few wounds here and there never stopped this rat." Now that Fletcher's belly was full, it became apparent that his costume had suffered far more abuse than his limbs. Napoleon's teeth must have nipped one of the stitches in the back center seam of his coat. The black cloth was now separated into two neat panels that flapped wildly about whenever Fletcher moved. It made him look more like a clown than a tap dancer.

"Benny, we need to find a good safe place to stay for a while," Ella said. "Our costumes need repair, our tap shoes need attention. We look more like a troupe of vagabonds than a dance act."

Benny nodded absentmindedly. His ear was cocked to the sound of someone singing. He motioned the rest to follow him down the hallway outside the Ratomat.

They found themselves in a busy passageway. Signs for the Rat Hollow Opera pointed in one direction, for the Glissade Ballet Company in another, and the Boom Boom Room in still another. Even though it was the middle of the night, Rat Hollow never seemed to close. Musicians hurried by carrying tubas and cello cases and violins. Girl rats with their tails coiled in ribboned twirls danced past, their chins lifted and their paws outstretched as if they were about to make an entrance onto the stage. A rotund rat with a bass voice was hawking the local rag, a newspaper called *Rat Hollow Rhythms*, which listed the latest audition times and dates. In the middle of it all, standing in front of a souvenir shop selling porcelain ballet slippers and miniature brass trumpets, stood a rat in baggy striped pants, red suspenders, and a vest. "Be sweet to your feet," he called out in a singsong voice as he executed a little soft-shoe routine and snapped his rag in time to his tune.

The Rattoons lined up to watch, and rats dodged around them, hurrying on their way.

"Now, there's a set of shoes that needs work," said the shoe-shine rat, pointing to Fletcher's scuffed toes. "Who's up first?" he asked, waving his paw across the row of high seats with their metal shoe posts.

The five settled happily into the empty chairs and watched the flow of musical rats go by as their new friend,

Buddy, filled them in on life in this particular section of the Hollow.

"Everybody comes here to dance and sing and make music. They're all waiting for the big break, the turn of the corner that will take them to the top. I seen them come, I seen them go. I stay here and I do the watching and the listening and I hear the sob stories." He shrugged in between snaps of his rag. "I know. I've walked the boards myself. And my father before me. Back then, my father and his friends used to set themselves up outside the big hotels with their shoe-shine kits. Minute they had a chance, they put down their rags and commenced to dance. Learned all my steps from him."

"Did you ever dance at the Boom Boom Room?" asked Ella.

"In my time. For a short while."

"You must have known Shadrach, then," said Woody.

"Sure enough. Everybody knows Shadrach. How's the old boy doing?"

"All right," said Benny guardedly.

"Still in that mash barrel, I suppose," said Buddy when he heard the tone in Benny's voice.

"Did you know Art and Sally?" asked Monk.

"Knowed about them. They were before my time. Legends, they were."

"Our parents," said Monk.

Buddy stopped his buffing for a minute and looked up

and down the row. "So you got music in your bones, I guess," he said.

"They opened the Boom Boom Room yet?" Woody asked.

Buddy shook his head. "Those new owners are a bunch of slackers. Went off to Florida and nobody knows when they'll be back."

"Could we get in there to see it?" asked Monk.

"No, sirree. Place is locked up as tight as a drum."

25

SETTLING IN

Buddy turned out to be a very helpful friend. Because of their heritage and his connections, he managed to move them into a cozy little apartment two blocks from the Boom Boom Room.

"Shadrach lived here for a while himself, so there's lots of your history in these walls. And besides that, you're going to be sleeping under one of the great legendary dance palaces in the country."

"What's that?" Ella asked.

"I mean aboveground. They have a show around this time every year. Humans travel from all over the world to see it. You ever heard of the Holiday Hullabaloo?"

"I saw a poster for it when we were coming in on the train that first day," Fletcher said.

"Buddy, you're talking about the Crystal, aren't you?" Benny asked. "The biggest dance palace in the whole world."

Buddy nodded, and their heads slowly rose to stare at the ceiling of their new place.

140

"How far up there is it?" Ella asked.

"A few levels. There's a tail opener that leads you right into the basement. Above the first *Boom* in the sign for the Room."

Benny clapped his paws over Fletcher's ears. "You didn't hear that, Fletch. Remember? No more trips aboveground."

Fletcher frowned. "Don't worry, Benny. Napoleon cured me."

"Does anybody ever go up there?" Monk asked.

"Some of the DFs. High command. There's a number of human restaurants in the area that provide food for the swanks down here. The ones who don't want to eat in the Ratomat."

"You ever been up there, Buddy?" Woody asked.

The rat looked uncomfortable and began to stare intently at his shoes. "Not to speak about," he mumbled under his breath.

"What does that mean?" Ella asked, but Benny elbowed her, and she fell silent.

Monk was busy sniffing around their new place. "It's perfect," he declared. "There's a rehearsal space out in the back, and the Ratomat's just down the block."

"Thought you'd take to it," said Buddy. "One more thing. Those tap shoes of yours could use some work. Go see Frankie at the Ratpaws."

"We know about him," Fletcher said. "Switchtail told us."

Buddy's eyes widened. "Switchtail? The creator of the Rat's Tail?"

"That's the one. He was our teacher," said Benny. "You know him?"

"I shook his paw once when he was coming off the dance floor." A note of awe had crept into Buddy's voice. "You Rattoons do have connections, I'll say that for you. Well, I've got to get back to my post. Come by and see me."

"We will," said Benny. "Thanks."

∘   •   ∘   •   ∘

Ella lost no time in organizing her troops. They were to be up at dawn. The breakfast visit to the Ratomat was allowed only after a full hour of stretches and warm-ups. Regular rehearsals were scheduled for ten and continued until four, with an hour's break for lunch.

In the evenings they strolled the streets of Rat Hollow, soaking up the atmosphere, stopping in cafés to listen to jazz, and watching the impromptu performances of street dancers. This section of the Hollow went to sleep singing and woke up tapping its feet. The very sidewalk thrummed, the lampposts pulsed with song, and the shutters rattled with the beat that seemed to roll out of the collective heart of a million committed musicians.

But love of music took its hostages, too. On many a street corner, you had to step over the sodden body of a failed drummer who had succumbed to the temptations of liquor or the sweet, smoky lure of a special kind of cigarette. Shadows cruised the edges of the buildings, burned-out rats who couldn't show their faces during the daytime anymore. Too many auditions, too many failures, too many visits to the Mash Barrel Blues, a club that kept the sweet liquid flowing night and day.

They made friends, too. A musician was happy to find any fellow music lover, whether their instruments were their feet or something held in their paws. The Rattoons felt more at home than they had in the barnyard. Their bones knew this place. It had been a part of them even before they were born. When word spread that Art and Sally's children had come to the Hollow, strangers pointed at them on the street and whispered to one another. Rats with graying whiskers and wise eyes would stop them in a café and shake their paws.

"Been nobody as good since Art and Sally cleared out of town," they'd say, scratching their heads and nodding to one another.

"So this is what took them away," said one large female who wore a flowered hat and sported a candy-striped cane. "Can't say as I blame them. You're a fine-looking litter. But we missed those two. Whenever they started up crooning, my feet would find themselves in a considerable disorder."

The five nodded and smiled and tried to be polite, but

these tributes began to wear on them after a while. How would they ever be as good as Art and Sally?

The comparison bothered Ella the most. She drove her brothers relentlessly. Now the rehearsals began at nine and most days stretched to five. Some nights they were too tired to stroll the streets but dropped like stones into their beds. Ella sat up, listening to them snore while she sketched out new combinations in her head. She was worried that their routines were tired and overused. Just the other morning in the Ratomat, she had overheard a conversation between two of the rats that she knew were planning to try out for the Boom Boom Room as soon as it reopened.

"I hear the owners are coming back in time for Christmas, and they want the Room to have a festive feel. They sent word they don't want any of our old routines. Something new and different," one said. "Something to excite them, give the place new life."

"Those owners don't know what they want," said the other. "Too much southern sun has fried their brains."

The first rat went right on talking. "I'm thinking of something with a Latin beat. Louie sent me word from down there that they've been hanging out at merengue joints. The Room is going to have a whole new energy. And we'd better be up to it." He poked his companion on the arm. "You watch out. They'll import some of those Miami rats, the ones straight off the boats from Cuba. We'll be out on our tails."

Latin beat, thought Ella. One of the foxes back at the barnyard had been talking about setting up a school for merengue and salsa dancing on the site of the old Blue Goat. But she couldn't find her way back to the barnyard now. There had to be some other solution.

26

THE SOLUTION

Late one afternoon, when the others had gone off to the Ratpaws to pick up their shoes from Frankie, Ella slipped away to see Buddy. He was resting in one of his chairs, perusing the latest copy of *Rat Hollow Rhythms*.

"You planning to get back in the business?" Ella asked with a sly grin.

"I keep my paw in," he said, folding up the paper. "How's by you?"

"I'm worried. We're good dancers, but we need some new routines, new life in the act. I hear the owners of the Boom Boom Room are coming back wanting a fresher beat to the dancing."

He shook his head. "Ella, the rumors that fly around here, you've got to ignore most of them. Did somebody send a rat runner down to Florida to check up on those owners? Of course not. It's just Rat Hollow gossip."

"Someone named Louie told these rats. I heard them talking about it in the Ratomat."

"I never heard of Louie. Pay no attention to that scuttlebutt."

He picked up the newspaper again, but when she didn't go away, he said, "Something else troubling you?"

"Tell me about the time you went aboveground. To the Crystal."

He looked around to be sure nobody had heard her.

"Best not to talk about that," he said.

"Come on, Buddy." She climbed up in the seat next to his and lowered her voice. "Tell me."

She could see him wrestling with himself. The battle didn't last long.

"Well," he said, leaning toward her. "That Crystal is the closest thing to heaven you might ever see. Now, don't get me wrong. I love it down here in Rat Hollow. But when you start talking scale and imagination, you have to hand it to those humans."

"What's it like?"

"When I say huge to you, you can't even understand what I'm telling you. It's the largest indoor theater in the world. The gold curtain alone weighs three tons."

"What's a ton?" Ella asked.

"I'm not sure, but I think if you put all the rats in Rat Hollow together, they wouldn't weigh anywhere near a ton. And this curtain weighs three. There are twenty-five thousand lights in the Palace. Six thousand humans can watch every show. But there's no way to picture it in your head. You'd have to see it for yourself." He clapped a paw over his mouth. "You didn't hear me say that."

"What kind of shows do they have?"

"Singers, dance acts, award ceremonies. Whatever you want."

Ella's ears pricked up. "Dancers?"

"The most famous in the human world. They're called the Sky Toes. Thirty-six precision line dancers onstage at one time."

"You ever seen them dance?"

"No, but I've seen them rehearse. They're probably at it right now." His eyes floated heavenward. "That Holiday Hullabaloo opens first week of November, so that means rehearsals started last week. I think of them all the time."

Ella giggled. "Buddy, you look like a rat in love."

He snapped the newspaper open so it covered his face.

She put a paw on his shoulder. "I was just kidding. Tell me more."

The paper rattled.

"Please, Buddy."

The paper lowered slowly.

"What do you want to know?"

"How do I get to see them?"

Buddy's eyes widened, and he looked left and right quickly. The passing rats were paying them no attention.

"You don't," he whispered.

"I'll go without you, then," she said.

"Go right ahead," said his voice from behind the paper again. "Suit yourself, sister."

Ella sat in silence. She hadn't really meant it when she said it, but the idea began to grow on her. If these Sky Toes were really that good, then she could learn some new combinations from them. They'd be just the ticket to putting juice into the Rattoons' act.

"Where did you say the tail opener comes out up there?" she asked thoughtfully.

"In the basement," he said.

"And where do they rehearse?"

"Ninth-floor hall. You'd never find it."

"Is that where you watched them?"

He didn't say anything.

"You found it. So why couldn't I?"

He was still pretending to read his paper, but Ella noticed that he was holding it upside down. She slid it out of his paws.

"I only need to see them once, Buddy. You know Switchtail said I was a promising choreographer, and I've been working on some new combinations. I've got to get a little help, a few new ideas."

"What about your brothers?"

"They wouldn't have to know. Imagine seeing the Sky Toes one more time, Buddy." He couldn't hide the excited gleam in his eyes. "Wouldn't you die happy if you could do that?"

He didn't answer. He didn't need to.

"When do we go?" she asked in a whisper.

"Day after tomorrow. Before dawn. Meet me here at six."

○　●　○　●　○

Ella announced a break in the rehearsal schedule. "We've been pushing too hard, and I need some time to work out my new combinations, so we're going to take Tuesday off."

"That's a relief," Fletcher said. "I'd begun to dance in my sleep. The same thing over and over. It was a nightmare."

Benny looked suspicious. "What are you going to do?"

She shrugged. "Research. Buddy says there's a good library in the Performing Rats Building. Those owners are going to be back from Florida any day, and we've got to be ready for them."

"Lay off, Benny," Woody said. "It's only one day." He'd begun courting Peggy, a ballet dancer in training for the Hollow Corps, and every minute he could, he slipped away to meet her at the Arabesque Café.

"All right," Benny said. "We've been going at it pretty hard."

"You're good at choreography, Ella," Fletcher said. "We've got all sorts of new routines that Switchtail doesn't even know."

"Sure," said Benny, patting his sister on the back. "Don't know what we'd do without you. You need a break yourself."

Ella shrugged and said nothing.

"Think I'll take that sight-seeing bus around the Hollow," said Benny. "I still haven't seen that statue of the Rat Hollow Founders that everybody talks about and the post office and the fairgrounds. Want to come, Fletcher?"

"Sure. There must be a museum somewhere in this town."

Monk was practicing a shim sham with the new rubber pads Frankie had put on all their shoes and didn't seem to be paying any attention.

27

ABOVEGROUND AGAIN

Ella woke at 5 A.M. and slid herself ever so carefully out of the warm pile of her brothers' bodies.

Buddy was pacing back and forth in front of his shoe stand. He'd hung a crudely lettered sign on one of the metal uprights that read, *Off for the day, see you tomorrow.*

"You're late," he said.

"No, I'm not. You're just nervous."

"Well, we've got to be upstairs in the rehearsal hall before 10 A.M. That's when they start."

"That's four hours from now—" She stopped speaking when he laid a paw on her shoulder.

"Someone's watching us," he whispered. "I'm sure I saw a rat duck into the shadows."

They peered around and waited. Nothing moved. The inviting smell of sour milk and rotting apples wafted out the door of the Ratomat, and from somewhere high above, Ella thought she heard the distant crash of a garbage can.

"Guess I was wrong," Buddy said. "Let's go."

They scuttled up over the awning and made their way to the top of the bright pink circle of the first *o* in the first *Boom*. Luckily the light in that letter had sputtered out some time ago, so they didn't have to worry that their bodies would be highlighted against a neon background. They balanced side by side while Buddy lifted his tail above his head and slipped the tip into the hole of the tail opener. The door swung open, and they clambered through.

"This is the basement of the Crystal," Buddy was whispering, but his voice seemed to bounce back at them from the long gray hallways. "It's the size of a city block, and it's easy to get lost down here. Now, let me see where I am." He closed his eyes and pressed a paw to one temple. "Straight down this hallway, they've got the stables for the animals they bring in for the holiday show."

"What animals?"

"Camels, donkeys, sheep. Stop interrupting. I'm thinking out loud. Right under the stage they have the elevators that take the band and the performers up for their numbers. Then there's the room with the hydraulic piston machine for running the elevators. Behind that, there's the elevator to the upstairs rehearsal halls. Okay, now I know where to go. Come on."

Behind them they heard a high-pitched squeak. A third rat was struggling to get the tip of his tail out of the tail opener. He pulled one more time and landed on his back with a thump. It was Monk.

"Oops, lost my footing there," he muttered as he got up

and dusted himself off. "Must be the new rubber pads. I'm not used to them yet."

"What are you doing here?" Ella growled. "And why are you wearing your tap shoes?"

"Breaking them in," he said with a sly smile. "You might say I'm just keeping an eye on my big sister. Performing Rats Library, my paw. I thought that whole story sounded pretty fishy."

"You sneaky little—"

Buddy hushed her. "He'll have to come along. There's no time to send him back. I smell humans."

Ella heard the musical clang of metal garbage cans, this time much closer, and then a door from the outside flapped open and a human trotted down the steps, whistling to himself. The rats melted into one of the shadowy corners and watched as the man disappeared around the corner.

"Stay close to me," Buddy whispered. "He's our ticket onto the elevator."

After a few more trips and a lot more off-key whistling, the maintenance man loaded one of the empty cans onto his dolly. The three rats slipped up next to the can and hung on for the long ride down the hallway.

"That's the stables," Buddy hissed into Ella's ear.

"What's behind all these doors?" she asked.

"It's a maze down here. They say even the humans get lost sometimes. Heating plant, electrical generators, music library, storage rooms, furniture-painting shops. This basement's gigantic, and it goes up four levels."

The dolly took an abrupt right turn. Monk slipped and lost his footing, but Buddy grabbed him by the scruff of his neck and the young rat managed to scramble back onto the metal platform.

The man took the elevator right up to nine, and as soon as he went whistling along the hallway to remove the trash, the three rats made a dash for the rehearsal hall door, which was cracked open. They slipped through and slid behind a pile of enormous alphabet blocks.

Buddy was panting. "Perfect timing. The dancers start drifting in early to warm up. Best to be in place."

"What are these things?" Ella asked, pointing at the oversized toys.

"Props for the show. The alphabet blocks are for the rag doll number. Gift boxes for under the tree."

"And those huge balls?"

"I bet they're supposed to be tree ornaments. Have to be big enough to see from the back row, I guess."

Monk's stomach began to growl. "You didn't bring any food, did you?" he whispered. "I didn't have time to stop at the Ratomat."

Ella glared at him. "If you'd minded your own business, you could be sitting there right now, happy as a rat in garbage."

Buddy waved at them to be quiet. The rehearsal door opened, and they heard the sound of human female voices.

It took a long time for the dancers to assemble, and there was a great deal of moaning about sore feet and the punishing schedule. It made Ella smile. She wasn't the only one having to drive her dancers to their limits.

The door opened once more, and the room went silent.

"Good morning, ladies," said a sharp female voice. "Everybody sleep well?"

There was a murmur from around the room.

"Good, then, let's not waste any more time. I don't expect you to start this morning at performance level, so you can mark it this first time. Maestro, play the piece through once, please."

The piano in the corner started the music. Ella poked her nose around one edge of an alphabet block while Buddy stood behind her. It was a sight to see. Thirty-six human females, seventy-two legs toeing the line, ears cocked to the music, arms around one another's waists. In the corner, the director conferred with a man who had a notepad while two or three other humans stationed themselves around the room to watch the dancers from every angle.

"We'll start where we left off yesterday with the tap number," called the rehearsal director. "Remember, it's a waltz piece, so everything will be in threes and sixes. If you're listening for the five, six, seven, eight beat, you're in the wrong rehearsal hall. Today we're going to work on the pullbacks. And a one and a two and a three."

The music filled the room, and the three rats stood transfixed as the long legs of the dancers lifted and turned and then, in perfect unison, the steel tips of their high-heeled shoes tapped the wooden floor. Above it all, the director counted and corrected.

"Head up, Leslie, four, five, six. Falap, shuffle, ball-change, heel. Stay in the four, five, six groove. Hold one, ball-change, step, falap. Drop your weight into that right foot, Amy. Jennifer, lift your arms. Good."

28

THE DANCE PALACE

They stayed until the lunch break. By that time, Monk was fainting from hunger, and Buddy had begun to worry that they would be discovered. Twice during the hourly breaks, they'd almost been caught. Once they had to pull Monk back from investigating one dancer's backpack, hoping for a candy bar. Another time a dancer had slipped behind one of the huge tree ornaments to wipe away tears of frustration. The rats dashed out of the way just before the human female slid to the floor, but she didn't seem to notice.

When lunch break was called, the three rats managed to melt into the river of dancers flowing toward the elevators. They hitched a ride on a rolling suitcase that parted from the rest and carried them down a long corridor. When it finally stopped in front of some swinging doors, they dropped off and looked around.

"Where are we?" Ella asked. "This isn't the basement level."

"The Great Chamber," Buddy said. He pointed to a chandelier that was hanging at least a mile above their heads. "Welcome to heaven, my friends."

On the wall, an enormous mural showed a human climbing a mountain into the clouds. The bronze balcony railings gleamed in the dim light, and the stair treads were carpeted in rich patterned wool. They couldn't take it all in. Monk turned around so many times with his snout in the air that he became quite dizzy.

"Since we're here and it's for the last time," Buddy said sternly, "I'll show you the Crystal Dance Palace. Take a deep breath, friends. I promise you won't ever see anything like this again in your lives."

They slipped through a crack between two swinging entrance doors and walked into the biggest theater in the world. It had the largest stage, the heaviest curtain, the highest ceiling, the greatest number of seats, and more spotlights than stars in the sky.

"Didn't I tell you?" Buddy asked. "Once I saw this, I figured I could die happy."

"Humans must like dancing too, then," said Ella. "To make this place just for hoofers like us."

Buddy spread his paws in reply. Monk tiptoed down the aisle toward the stage.

"Can you imagine tapping on that stage?" he said in awe.

"Nobody would ever see us," Ella said.

"Yes, they would." Buddy pointed to two enormous projection screens on either side of the gold curtain. "People in the very last row could see a fly doing somersaults on a bottle cap. You build a place this big, you gotta make sure the fans leave happy. And they do."

"How do you know?" Ella asked.

"Sometimes I can hear them down in the Hollow. Just the faintest sound of humans cheering and the stomping of feet. For the longest time I thought I was dreaming it. Until I saw this. Then I knew."

Monk was scampering across the tops of the seats in one of the rows. "You ought to see the view from here, Ella."

"All right, Monk, time for us to split," Buddy said, and just at that moment, they heard the sound of a human voice.

"Get down," Ella squeaked, and Monk dropped through the space between the seat and the floor. The other two crouched in the aisle and waited. The voice came nearer. It appeared to be half singing, half talking to itself.

"First one tells me to clean out the camel pen, then the other sends me up here with the razor. How's a person to know who's in charge in this place?" Then the man dropped to his knees between the seats in one row. His voice dropped with him until it sounded as if it were rumbling up out of a sewer.

"Monk, come on," Ella said, her voice edgy.

"I can't," squeaked Monk. "I'm stuck."

Buddy and Ella tiptoed down the aisle until they found Monk's row. "Stuck in what?" Buddy asked.

"I don't know," said Monk. "Some kind of gray mud."

The two looked down the line of seats to where Monk was trapped.

"Oh no," Buddy said, his voice grim. "It's gum. He's got himself stuck in a wad of gum."

"What is it?"

"Some disgustingly sweet stuff that humans chew until it loses its taste. Then they spit it out all over the place. It's on the sidewalks and in phone booths and on the backs of signs. The DFs have special training before they go aboveground to learn how to avoid gum."

"I can't move my feet," Monk moaned. "It's like quicksand."

"Stay calm," Ella called. "We'll figure this out." She turned to Buddy. "They bring the stuff into a place like this?" she asked.

"Sure. There's no accounting for humans. They stick it up under the seats and all over the floor. Someone told me they take twenty pounds of gum out of here every day." Buddy clapped a paw to his forehead. "That guy must be the gum scraper."

"You mean they stick this junk on everything and then they pay someone to take it up? That doesn't make any sense."

Suddenly the man appeared at the other end of Monk's row and began to walk right toward him.

"Out of sight," Buddy whispered, and gave Ella a shove.

"Well, now, what do we have here?" the man asked himself when he caught sight of Monk. He was holding a tool that looked like a small spatula in his right hand. "I'd say, old boy, that you are trapped like a rat." He put his head back and roared at his own joke while Monk tried to make himself as small as possible. "You are in a regular pickle, aren't you, now?" The raucous laughter stopped suddenly, and the human voice dropped to a low, threatening tone. "Nothing I hate more than a slimy, dirty, garbage-eating rat messing up the place. You know what this is?" he asked. "This here's a razor. It's meant to scrape gum off the floor. But this time I got a better use for it," he said as he dragged one grimy forefinger across his own throat.

Monk shot Ella a terrified look.

"Get ready to charge him," Buddy whispered to Ella as he dropped into attack position. "Go right for his face if you have to."

· 29 ·

THE REſCUER

Just then, the swinging door at the back of the room opened with a loud squeak and a voice called out.

"Rosco, you in here?"

"Damn," the man muttered in a low voice that only the rats could hear. "First Blunt, now this one. Why don't they leave me be?"

"Rosco?"

"Right here, boss," the man answered. "I got a nasty-looking rat stuck in a wad of gum. Just going to take care of him."

"Don't touch him," barked the voice suddenly. "Stand up so I can see you."

With one more menacing wave of his razor at Monk, Rosco got reluctantly to his feet. "What's wrong, boss?"

"You're supposed to be downstairs, cleaning out that camel's pen. I told you that this morning, didn't I?"

"Yeah, but Mr. Blunt said I had to do the gum detail 'cuz Tony didn't come to work today."

The tall man with the commanding voice had made his way down to their row. "I'm your boss, Rosco, not Blunt. Give me the razor and get downstairs."

"What about this here rat?"

"I'll take care of him," said the boss. "Get going."

Rosco mumbled something under his breath.

"What did you say, Rosco?"

"Nothin', boss, nothin'."

"He called him a rat lover," Buddy whispered to Ella.

Nobody moved until they heard the swinging door squeak again. The man stared at Monk for a moment and then down the row to where Buddy and Ella were hiding behind the last seat.

"You can come out now," he said. "I have no intention of harming you."

"You speak our language," Buddy said in awe.

"You must be the one Switchtail told us about," said Ella.

"Oliver String Bean Bailey," Monk cried. "It's him."

"The very one," said Mr. String Bean Bailey as he settled himself into the seat closest to Monk. "I'm honored that you have heard something of me, that I have in some way entered the annals of rat history. Please call me Oliver."

"Barney the rat taught you our language, didn't he?" said Ella.

"That he did. First ancient ratspeak and then the modern everyday. Barney was a tough teacher."

"What does ancient ratspeak sound like?" Buddy asked.

Oliver closed his eyes for a minute. "I would beseech you to show yourselves so that I may make your better acquaintance. How's that?"

"Strange," said Monk.

"I am pretty rusty. Not much opportunity to practice," said Oliver as he knelt on the floor, razor blade in hand. "Now, let's see what we can do about your predicament."

Buddy and Ella crept closer. "You'd better not hurt my brother," she cried.

"I have no intention of harming a hair on his head. You can come guard him if you like. What do you call yourself?" Oliver asked.

"Monk," said Monk.

"Well, now," he said, "that's a suitable name for a rat in tap shoes. And yours?" he asked Ella, meaning to distract her as he slid the razor blade in between Monk's right tap shoe and the floor with one swift and practiced flick of his wrist. Monk's foot snapped free so suddenly that he staggered about for a moment.

"Watch it, sailor," the man said as he placed a forefinger behind the rat's back to steady him. Then he wrapped his hand gently about Monk's waist and settled into his seat with Monk in his lap. "Got to get every scrap of gum off these shoes or you'll go head over heels when you commence your tapping." He leaned over and looked at the other two. "You can join us up here if you wish."

Buddy and Ella scampered up the side of the seat and perched on the armrest. "And you're wearing jazz shoes, I can see," Oliver said with a glance at Ella's feet. "So you're part of a troupe. How many are there?"

"Five," she said. "We call ourselves the Rattoons."

He nodded his approval. "Not a bad name." Monk was so relaxed by this time that his head was lolling over the edge of the man's knee.

"I'm Buddy. I'm not part of the Rattoons," Buddy said. "I'm a shoe-shine rat."

"An honorable calling. There you go, young rat," he said, setting Monk down on the floor. "Try a pullback."

Monk did.

"No sticking?"

"No sticking," Monk said.

"Those are good shoes. The rubber pads are useful on rough surfaces."

"You know a lot about dance," said Buddy.

"I've been managing acts my whole life. Dancers, circus shows, singers—you name it."

"Like the Acrobrats," said Ella.

"That group, too," said Oliver. "Until they disappeared on me. Went back down to the Hollow, I suspect."

"They didn't go willingly," said Monk. "They were arrested. For being aboveground without a permit."

"Which is exactly what's going to happen to us any minute," said Buddy. "We got to get out of here."

"That's right," Ella said. "Or I'll forget the combinations I learned this morning."

"And I'll be dead from hunger," Monk gasped.

Oliver put up his hands. "Hold on, what's the scurry and scramble? We might have a little business to talk over."

"Business?" said Ella.

"Just to put you straight on my current situation, I'm managing the animals for the Holiday Hullabaloo, but there's no talent in that group. They shuffle on the stage, stare at the audience, and shuffle off again. I've been looking for a new dance troupe. And here you are."

"Listen, Mr. String Bean Bailey," Buddy said. "Right now, we are traveling aboveground without any papers or permission. It is completely illegal, and we are never going to do this again. Right, Ella?"

"Right," she said, although her voice wavered for a moment. "We just came to see the Sky Toes. I'm figuring out some new combinations for our audition. That's all we Rattoons want to be—the best dancers the Boom Boom Room has ever seen."

"And of course, the Boom Boom Room is down in the Hollow."

They nodded.

"So don't go tempting these young rats with any schemes," Buddy warned. "Just pop us in the elevator and take us downstairs and we won't bother you again."

"Although we were very glad to meet you," Monk added. "After all we've heard."

Oliver looked resigned. "Then will you do me one favor before you go? Will you dance for me on the big stage,

Monk? Strut your stuff for the one human who would truly appreciate your talent."

Monk looked at Ella. He hated turning down any invitation to show off his tap, especially on a stage as big as this one.

"Is that a threat, Mr. String Bean Bailey?" Buddy asked. "Are you saying you won't let us go unless Monk dances?"

"No, Mr. Buddy, I don't work that way. I'm saying I'm never going to see him dance down in the Hollow, so he should give me a chance here."

"All right," said Ella. "This one time. Although I don't know how he'll ever hear the beat over the growling in his stomach."

"I can do it," said Monk.

30

MONK'S PERFORMANCE

Oliver lifted all three rats onto the enormous stage. Monk did some quick stretches and then backed off a little to give himself room. Oliver disappeared for a minute and then returned with a boom box.

"This belongs to the tech crew. They use it on their lunch break. I picked out a tape of old swing songs. What do you want?"

"'Fascinating Rhythm,'" Ella said. "Have you got that?"

"Right here," said Oliver, and he cued it up.

"You remember the combination, don't you, Monk?" Ella called across the stage to him. "Brush, step, step, shuffle, ball-change—"

Monk put up his paw. "I know, I know, Ella. Leave me alone."

He was hungry of course, a little stiff from his time in the pool of gum, and awed by the size of the space. He might as well have been dancing on a stage at the top of the world, but he forced himself to keep his mind on his feet and the crisp snap of the toe taps against the wooden floor. And soon, as often happened when he was performing, Monk lost himself in the rhythm, in the happy marriage of his tapping with the beat of the music. At the end, he took a bow and, when Oliver continued to clap, another one.

"You are good," Oliver said.

Monk wasn't sure how to respond, so he bowed a third time.

"Bailey," a voice sounded from the back of the huge room.

When Oliver turned around to search for the source of the voice in the dark interior, the three rats slipped into the shadow of his broad back.

"Right here, Blunt."

"Where's Rosco? I sent him up here to scrape gum."

"I needed him downstairs to clean the camel's pen."

"You know, Bailey, I give that man his orders. And I don't like someone going against me on that."

"Animals can't wait. Gum can," said Oliver in a quiet voice.

"We'll see about that," said Blunt. He turned on his heel and slammed out of the room. The swinging door took a while to stop moving.

"Are you in trouble?" Buddy asked.

"When it comes to other humans, I usually am," Oliver said with a sigh.

He gave them a ride down to the basement in his pockets.

"Oliver, are you down here most of the time?" Ella asked.

"Every day, keeping an eye on my clients." He jerked his head over his shoulder. "One donkey, six sheep, and a camel. They may not have much talent, but they deserve the best treatment, just like all my clients."

"Think you could get me up to the ninth floor on the elevator if I ever needed to go back?"

"Ella, you're not coming back aboveground no matter what," Buddy said. "It's too dangerous."

Ella ignored him. "Could you, Oliver?"

"Sure. I don't have a regular office, but I'm here by nine most mornings. I can usually be found down the hall. Room has a *B* on the door."

"So maybe someday, we'll meet again," Ella said.

Oliver gave her a formal little bow. "I would be honored, Miss Ella Rattoon," he said. "I pray you will walk in health and fortune."

"Ancient ratspeak," said Monk.

"Well, you take care of yourself, too, Oliver," said Ella, who felt suddenly shy.

Buddy walked over to the tail opener and signaled to the others to follow.

31

THE AUDITION

To Buddy's dismay, Ella snuck aboveground one or two more times. She always picked Tuesday, which had become the Rattoons' official day off. Monk, of course, knew where she was going, but the others never suspected. She was putting them through so many new routines that they were grateful for the break.

"Where's she getting all this stuff?" Benny asked late one Tuesday morning in the Ratomat.

Monk kept his head down, which wasn't hard because he'd snagged a bowl of macaroni with deliciously rancid cheese.

"She's a creative genius," said Fletcher. "An artist in her own way."

"That's true," said Benny. "But I wish she wouldn't push herself so hard."

"Monk, stop that awful slurping," Woody said. "It's enough to put me off my feed."

"The Chinese rat slurps on purpose," he said. "It's considered polite. Shows he's enjoying his food."

"The things you kids are learning in the Hollow," said Benny. "Yesterday I heard Ella having a long conversation with a DF about the dangers of chewing gum aboveground. Now, how would she know anything about that?"

"We're not kids," Monk said. "You're only a couple of years older than us, Benny, so you don't need to act so high and mighty."

○　●　○　●　○

Ella barely slept. She danced her way up and down the streets of the Hollow, trying out the steps she had learned in the ninth-floor rehearsal hall and stringing them into combinations of her own. She taught her brothers a new way to do pullbacks so their bodies looked weightless and they didn't always have to start from a flat-footed position. She drilled them on the Shim Sham Shimmy and then taught them the Suzie Q. She worked them hard on their time steps and pushed them to move off the balls of their feet. They found entirely new muscle groups in their legs. In the evenings, Benny and Woody made regular trips to the public baths, where they soaked for hours in the steamy, bubbling water.

The following week Ella concentrated on jazz. She rechoreographed the dances they did to their parents' recordings. Out of her mouth, she heard the words of the director aboveground. "Let those shoulders slip, Monk. Loosen your hips, Woody. Looser than that. Drop the

173

shoulders even more. Your body needs to look like rubber. Benny, when you're turning, hold your head still till the last possible moment. Make that whip of the head as crisp as your tap shoe spanking the floor."

Then she began to work them through a routine set to a special jazz rendition of a Christmas medley.

"When the owners come back, they're going to want a holiday show. Bet nobody else auditioning is thinking of that," said Ella.

"Bet they all are," drawled Fletcher.

"Those owners had better hurry up," said Benny. "The holidays will be come and gone before they ever return."

One day, Monk came tearing around the corner from an afternoon snack at the Ratomat.

"They're back," he said. "The lights are on in the sign, and there's an audition notice out front."

"When?" Ella asked.

"Friday at one o'clock. Everyone in the Ratomat was talking about it."

"We're going to station someone there at six in the morning."

Of course, everybody had the same idea. By 6 A.M., when the Rattoons arrived for the audition, there were thirty dancers ahead of them. The ones at the front of the line had spent the night there.

Ella put their names on the list. They left Monk holding their place in line. The rest of them went home for one last rehearsal.

Finally Benny decided they'd had enough. "Ella, you're going to kill yourself if you keep pushing like this. Relax."

"Easy for you to say," she spat. "What if we don't make it into the Boom Boom Room? It will be my fault."

"No, it won't. And it won't be the end of the world either."

"Calm down, sister," said Woody. "You're wound up tighter than a top."

It was true. She hadn't slept in days. How could a rat sleep when a million digs and turns and shuffles and falaps were dancing through her head, a hundred tunes and snatches of songs playing themselves out in her dreams? Benny took over, finished the rehearsal, and then they went to join Monk in the line.

"Good you came back," he gasped. "I was going to send a runner for you."

"What's happened?" asked Fletcher.

"They're throwing people out in the middle of their first numbers. Only two groups ahead of us now."

"Have they hired anybody?" Ella asked.

"They're not saying. But most of the ones coming out look pretty bad, and a lot of them are heading across the street right into the Mash Barrel Blues."

A tall rat in a blue cap threw open the door, shouted a name off his clipboard, and ushered in two dancers in sequined costumes. Five minutes later the sequins were out, four rats with berets had gone in, and the Rattoons were first in line.

"Everybody take a deep breath," Benny said. "No matter what happens in there, we're good and we know it. We may not be what they want, but we're still good."

The door slapped open again, the four berets slunk away, and the tall rat shouted, "RATTOONS."

He led them down a gloomy corridor into a small, ill-lit rehearsal studio. The dust had been swept into the corners, and it blew about every time the doors opened. The place smelled dank and unused. Two rats in caps sat on director's chairs, with a flashlight shining on papers on the table in front of them. They barely looked up when the Rattoons filed in.

"Brought your own music?" one yelled.

"Yes, sir," Woody said. "Right here."

"Get it going. We don't have all day."

The Rattoons glanced at one another and then took their places in the line. Ella and Woody had picked a jazz rendition of "Deck the Hollow." Ella had taught her brothers the long jazz arm movements and shifting shoulders she had learned aboveground.

The music began, the familiar notes of the Christmas tune with the snappy embellishments of horn and percussion. The Rattoons had barely moved into their second combination when one of the rats in back called out, "Stop."

Woody pressed the stop button on the machine.

"You got nothin' else? We don't want Christmas music."

Ella's eyes widened. "But we thought—"

"We don't care what you thought, lady. Snap, bring on the next group."

"We've got something else," Benny shouted. "Just give us a minute."

"That's about all the time we got, mister. One minute. You see that line of dancers waiting out there?"

"This isn't fair," Ella shouted. "This is no way to audition dancers."

"Zip the lip, lady, and get those feet moving."

Monk fast-forwarded to one of their old tunes, Art's version of "Rat Alley." Ella was so furious that she missed the first count and started on the wrong foot. This threw off Woody, who bumped into Fletcher, which made him stumble.

The rat in the back stood up and threw down his pencil. "Get these losers out of here, Snap. Who wants to watch a bunch of country rats crashing into each other?"

"We wouldn't work for you if you offered us center stage seven nights in a row," Ella shouted. "This is the most unprofessional business I have ever witnessed. You could learn a thing or two from upstairs if you took the time."

"Upstairs? What are you talking about?" the rat yelled back. "You been aboveground or something? Got transit papers?"

"Nothing," Monk said. "She's not talking about anything."

"Don't yell at my sister," said Benny. "Or I'll come up there and flatten that smart snout of yours."

The shouting match went on as Snap ushered the Rattoons off the stage.

32

ELLA'S CRAZY IDEA

In a very short time, the five Rattoons found themselves outside, blinking in the bright afternoon light. Snap was bellowing the name of the next group.

"What was it like?" asked a young rat from her place in the line.

"Do you think you got the job?" said her partner.

"How many are they taking?" called a rat.

"They're crooks," yelled Ella. "I don't think they're hiring anybody."

The crowd began to buzz.

"They wouldn't know a good dancer from a snake," she carried on. "They wouldn't know—" She was cut off in midsentence when Woody and Fletcher lifted her and bore her away down the street. Her shoes barely grazed the top of the cobblestones.

"Put me down," she cried. "Those rats are lazy good-for-nothings. They're not going to pick any of us. They just enjoy torturing us."

"Ella," Benny said sternly, once her brothers had gotten her out of earshot. She went on yelling. "Ella," he said, a little louder. Finally she subsided into silence. The four brothers stood staring at her.

"Well, I'm right, aren't I?"

"You may be right, but all that carrying on didn't help one bit. That's it for the Boom Boom Room," Fletcher said. "Our days there are finished."

"We don't want to dance there anyway," Ella said. "I'll never set foot in that place again."

"Ella," Benny said once more, and the eerie quiet of his voice unnerved her.

"What?" she said, a little too loudly.

"What did you mean when you said they could learn a thing or two from upstairs?"

She looked at her feet, tried to rub a spot off her right jazz shoe with her left. "Nothing," she mumbled.

He took her chin in his paw and lifted it. "Nothing?" he said.

The other three shifted back and forth on the cobblestones.

"You've been picking up all these combinations, these new steps from books in the Performing Rat Library? Why don't I believe that?"

"All right," she shouted with a stomp of her foot. "I went aboveground. To the Sky Toes rehearsal hall on the ninth floor."

"How many times?" Benny asked.

"A couple. Two or three. What's the problem with that? I didn't get caught, did I?"

"It was amazing," said Monk in a dreamy voice.

They whirled on him. "You went too?"

"Just once," he said.

"Benny," Fletcher said. "Best we move along." A little crowd had gathered around them. "Take care of this business at home."

○　●　○　●　○

In the end, Monk and Ella spilled it all. Buddy and the Sky Toes and the gum trap and meeting the famous Oliver String Bean Bailey.

Benny looked pale. "You trusted a human?" he asked, his voice barely a squeak.

"Benny, it's Oliver Bailey. Remember what Switchtail said about him? He's not like the others," Monk said.

"Switch wasn't even sure he believed those stories."

"But Oliver speaks our language," Ella said. "And ancient ratspeak too."

"Buddy said he'd never heard anything like it," Monk added.

"Wait till I get ahold of Buddy," Benny muttered.

"It wasn't his fault. It was mine," Ella said proudly. "He didn't want to go. I forced him to do it. And our dancing did get better. You have to admit that."

"She's right," Fletcher said. "Much better."

"You of all rats," Benny roared, turning on his brother. "The one who almost had his spine snapped by Napoleon? Do you realize she could have been squashed flat, poisoned, dropped down an elevator shaft, run over by a dolly, electrocuted, burned in an incinerator. . . ." He ran out of breath and horrible ideas at the same time.

"I didn't think of all those things," Ella said.

"No, of course you didn't. I'm the one who does all the thinking around here. And I've made up my mind. We have to face facts. We're not ever going to dance at the Boom Boom Room. We're finished in the Hollow, so we're going back to the barnyard, where I know we'll be safe."

The uproar was instantaneous. A chorus of furious siblings turned on Benny.

"You can go wherever you want, Benny—"

"I'm staying here—"

"I'm not leaving Peggy for anything—"

"You don't tell us what to do."

Benny didn't speak, and the rest of them wound down.

"So what are you all intending to do?" he finally asked.

"Stay right here," Woody said. "Peggy and I are thinking of entering a ballroom-dance competition."

"Look for other gigs," said Monk. "The Room isn't the only act in town."

"Take up painting," Fletcher said. "If the humans won't paint rats, then I think one of our species should show them how it's done. I had this thought the other day. Art. Rat. Same letters, just rearranged."

Monk groaned.

"You're on your own, then," said Benny. "I'll be celebrating Christmas in the barnyard."

"Benny," Monk cried. "You want to break up the act? We're all in this together. The five Rattoons."

"We came here to dance at the Boom Boom Room, remember? We're not ever going to do that, not so long as those two lowlifes own the place. So that tells me it's time to go home." He shrugged. "I miss the barnyard, the sweet tickle of hay under my head at night. . . . Nothing wrong with that."

They stood in shocked silence. The four Rattoons? Benny gone? How could this be possible?

"I've got an idea," said Ella. "We should celebrate Christmas together, Benny. Then if you still want to, you can go home after that. And I've got a barnyard we can celebrate in."

"Where?" said Fletcher.

Her eyes moved upward. "They brought in the animals for the Holiday Hullabaloo a couple of weeks ago."

"What animals?" Woody asked.

"Sheep, a camel, a donkey. They have their own stables. The keepers take them up onto the stage on an enormous elevator."

"She means aboveground." Benny shook his head. "In the Crystal."

"You've got to see this place at least once," Ella said to Benny, her voice suddenly urgent. "Tell them, Monk."

"Buddy says it's the closest thing to heaven, and he's right. It's the largest dance hall in the world." Monk twirled once and then again. "I danced on the stage for Oliver. I bet it's as big as all of Rat Hollow. The curtain is gold, and there are six thousand seats and two huge screens."

"You know, Fletcher, how you felt about the museum?" Ella asked. "Well, that's the way I feel about this place." She went on, describing the Great Chamber, the nine-foot chandeliers lowered to the floor for cleaning, the plush carpeting, the miles of seats, the enormous murals, and it wasn't long before the others became interested.

"Any pictures of rats?" Fletcher asked.

"I haven't seen any," Ella said, "but the place is so big, I'm sure there's one somewhere."

"What would Peggy think if I told her I'd seen a place like that?" Woody mused.

"She'd have you arrested," groaned Benny.

"Just once, Benny," Ella said. "It would be our Christmas treat. Snuggle in some hay. Sing some carols. And I bet Oliver would get us upstairs so you could see the Dance Palace itself. Then you could die happy, I promise you that."

"I'd die happy knowing we were headed back to the barnyard," he said, but from the tone of his voice, they could tell he was weakening.

"So you agree, Benny?" Monk asked. "One trip aboveground."

"No talk of leaving until after that?" said Fletcher.

"Let's go tomorrow," Ella said. Before we lose our nerve, she thought.

Benny threw up his paws. "What choice do I have with the four of you against me? But that's it. One more trip aboveground and then we go home, right?"

They all nodded solemnly, but many a paw was crossed behind their backs.

33

THE BAƒEMENT OF THE CRYƒTAL

Even at nine in the morning, the basement level of the Crystal was a madhouse of activity.

The rats hunkered down in a shadowy corner out of the way.

"This is bedlam," whispered Fletcher. "What's going on?"

"The Holiday Hullabaloo," Ella said. "Oliver told me they put on four shows a day."

"So many humans," said Benny, wrinkling his nose.

"Too many to pay any attention to us," Monk said gamely, although he wasn't exactly sure. The scent of them was overwhelming.

"Follow me," Ella said.

They found Oliver in the room with the *B* on the door. He was leaning against a bulletin board, giving Rosco his orders for the morning. Oliver's eyes widened at the sight of so many of them, and he gave Ella a nod that she understood. She herded her brothers behind the door and they waited.

As soon as Rosco had left, Oliver closed the door and leaned against it.

"You can come out now, Miss Ella. And good morning to yourself, Monk."

"You see what I mean," Ella whispered to Benny. "He speaks our language. And he's nice."

"Aren't you going to introduce me to your other brothers, Ella?"

"Oliver, this is Fletcher, Woody, and Benny. Benny's the oldest."

The three bowed politely but kept their distance.

"Pleased to meet you all. I have to tell you, you couldn't have come at a worse time for the rehearsal hall," said Oliver. "Far too much traffic in the elevators. I'm not sure I have enough pockets for the five of you."

"Not to worry, Oliver," Ella assured him. "We don't need the rehearsal hall today. I just wanted to show the boys around. Take them down to the stables. Maybe later a quick trip up to the Dance Palace."

He shook his head. "I'll do my best, but it's going to be rough. You know once the show starts, the Sky Toes come down here a couple of times. Sometimes they go up the same way, but other times they cross over to go up in the other elevator. Not to mention the orchestra and my pack of clients milling around for their big Nativity scene. It's a regular Grand Central Station down here."

"It already is," said Benny.

"You can ride in Rosco's pouch," Oliver said, taking it down from a hook. "He doesn't do any gum scraping till the afternoon between shows."

Monk looked suspicious. "No leftover gum in there, Oliver?"

The man turned it inside out and showed him. "Clean as a whistle. Brand-new issue this week. Only been used once, I believe."

Ella and Monk were the first to crawl inside. The others followed reluctantly, screwing up their noses against the smell of human and a sickly sweet odor they couldn't quite place.

Oliver let them out at the entrance to the stable. "I'll be back to check on you when I can," he said. "You'll have a front-row seat for all the to-ings and fro-ings, the comings and goings, but do keep your precious snouts out of sight, won't you?"

"See?" Ella asked Benny as Oliver disappeared around the corner. "He's everything Switch said he was."

Benny nodded. A human with a respect for rats. It truly was a wonder.

34

THE DANCE OF THEIR LIVES

The donkey and the sheep sniffed curiously at the new arrivals.

"You part of the show?" they asked.

"Oh no," said Ella. "Just observers. How's it going?"

"Would be fine if it weren't for that lousy camel," said the donkey, whose name was Coleman. "He spits when you least expect it. Nasty habit."

"They have to send him up to the stage with his handler while the rest of us are led by members of the cast," said one of the sheep. "No stage presence, that camel. No training. Don't know how he got in the show."

"Mind if we look around?" Benny asked.

"No problem. Make yourselves at home. All the hay and water and food you'd ever want. It's a peachy life. Mr. Bailey, our manager, sees to that."

"You like him?" Monk asked.

"Best in the business. He makes sure they take good care of us." The donkey glanced over his shoulder at Rosco, who was forking up the straw in the sheep's pen with a handkerchief tied over his nose. "He keeps an eye on that guy, who's nothing but trouble."

"You can say that again," said Monk.

"Listen, he's better than that man Blunt. The one who thinks he's such a big shot," said Coleman. "He wants to use humans dressed up as animals for the Nativity. Then he could get rid of us and Oliver at the same time."

○　●　○　●　○

The four boys dove into a pile of straw and rolled around in it, tossing it up and then at one another. Ella paid them no attention. She was perched at the front edge of the sheep's pen, watching the activities.

Members of the orchestra swept by, pulling on their coats and calling to one another. Two workers pushed a cartload of costumes to the basement changing room, followed by a seamstress with a dress hanging over one arm and a pincushion in the other hand. The ushers ducked in and out of the cafeteria, some eating on the run. From the hall above came the sounds of instruments tuning up, the faint tapping of feet, and the rolling of wheels across the stage.

"Do the Sky Toes come down here?" Ella asked a sheep.

"Yep. A couple of times."

"Which numbers are they doing?"

"Can't keep them all straight," she said. "If you told me some names, I might remember."

"'Rock Around the Christmas Tree,' 'Mistletoe Jazz'—"

"That one," she said. "They definitely do 'Mistletoe Jazz.'"

"We know 'Mistletoe Jazz,'" Ella said to Monk. "I called it 'Rat Tree Jazz,' but it's got a lot of the same combinations. You remember?" She took off her tap shoes and walked through the first steps.

"Sure," he said, and joined her, humming under his breath.

"Dancing rats," said the sheep. "Now I've seen everything." The animals crowded around to watch when the other three slipped out of their shoes. Monk hummed, and Ella counted it out. Her brothers fell into step.

The sheep bleated. The donkey brayed his approval. The camel called from his pen to ask what was going on, but nobody bothered to answer him.

"Too bad they didn't audition you before they signed on that one," said a sheep with a toss of his head.

Ella and the rest dropped to the floor to put on their tap shoes.

"You do tap, too?" asked the smallest sheep.

"Show 'em, Monk," said Benny. He cleared the hay off to make a small stage.

Monk jumped to his feet and did a quick shim sham.

Woody bounced his brother off the floor with a Suzie Q.

Fletcher entered from the side with a Double Buggy Rat Tail.

Ella and Benny came at each other from opposite sides and finished with a Tack Ratty.

"Now, that's dancing," said the largest sheep, who had pushed his way to the front.

"Would someone tell me what you're all looking at?" called the camel.

"Where'd you learn how to dance like that?" asked one of the sheep, but before anybody could answer, Coleman put up his hoof. "The show's starting," he said. All eyes lifted and if they strained, they could just hear the opening notes on the organ.

"We're the last number," Coleman said. "We've got some time."

"How do you get up there?" Benny asked.

"The elevators. They put us on when they bring the Sky Toes down to make their crossover."

"Where are the elevators?" Woody asked.

"End of each hall," bleated a sheep with a nod of her woolly head. "Amazing contraptions."

They watched as the traffic in the hallways ebbed and flowed, depending on the action upstairs. Oliver rushed by at one point, but he only had time to wave in their general direction.

Suddenly from the far end of the hall there came an enormous whirring sound.

"What's that?" Ella asked.

"The elevator," Coleman said. "They're bringing down the Sky Toes. They go back up on the same one this time after a costume change." He pointed to a program with his right hoof.

"Oh, look, the third song is 'Mistletoe Jazz,'" Ella cried. "And they're going to do 'Rock Around the Christmas Tree.' We know that one, too. Come on," she said to the boys. "I want you to see them."

There was no time to argue before she was over the side of the pen and scampering down the hall. The brothers followed, hugging the wall and dodging out of the way of feet, boxes, dollies, and costume racks.

The line of thirty-six dancers broke as the elevator touched down. They filed off in order and were immediately surrounded by a crowd of dressers carrying short red skirts and gold shoes for the next song. The buzz of conversation rose like a cloud above the uplifted arms and the swish of silk in the air.

"You have to see them dance," said Ella to Benny. "They're amazing, like nothing else in the world. I know where we can watch them. Follow me," she said, and was off again. She led them around the edges of a small room where they could hear humans talking.

"What's in there?" Woody asked.

"It's the control room for the elevator. Last time I was here, Oliver gave me a tour. If we go up over the top, we can hop onto the elevator."

"Ella," Benny cried, but she shook her head and started off again.

By the time the Sky Toes filed back to the elevator,

smoothing their skirts and adjusting their white fur hats, the five rats were hiding under the front row of rising steps between the mighty hydraulic pistons that lifted them up and the choral staircase. Above their heads, the rats heard the tap-tap-tapping of seventy-two heels as the dancers climbed to their assigned places.

"Ella, how will we ever get down again?" Fletcher asked.

"We'll ride back down when the elevators come to get the donkey and the sheep. This is perfect. You can see the Dance Palace and the Sky Toes dancing at the same time."

The whirring started up again, this time beneath them, and the floor shuddered as they rose the twenty-seven feet up to the stage level. The sound of the orchestra grew louder and louder until the Rattoons felt as if they had moved right inside the tuba. From above their heads, they could hear again the tap of feet, but this time the heels were lifting and falling to the tune the orchestra was playing.

When she thought back on it later, Ella couldn't explain what exactly happened to her in that moment. The orchestra was playing "Rock Around the Christmas Tree," a song she had heard in her sleep, she had danced to down the streets of the Hollow on her way home from her secret trips to the ninth floor.

Her feet began to talk to her, and she followed where they led, out around the corner of the riser and onto the stage. And where she went, her brothers went. Like all great tap dancers, they had to obey the call of their bodies, and the music begged them to come, to join in, to fill in the spaces between the horn and the piano. Before they knew it, they had moved into center stage and the cameras had picked them up and projected them onto the seventy-foot screens.

The audience gasped, one single release of breath. The Sky Toes dancing on the choral staircase above the Rattoons couldn't see what the people were staring at but kicked their legs even higher in response. The horn players picked up the energy moving through the hall and blew it out their horns. The piano player pounded it into his keys. The drummer put aside his sticks so the tappers could take his place.

This was the dance of their lives, and they knew it. It was certain they would never live to dance again, and so they gave it everything they had. All the training and rehearsals, all the counting in their sleep, all the steps they had ever learned right back to Switchtail and the barnyard, back before that to those nights under the table at the Blue Goat when the music flowed through their blood and their muscles and into their bones. They danced clean and strong and sharp, and every kiss of their taps against the stage was magnified a thousand times by the speakers and carried to the very back rows of the enormous hall.

When the dance was finally over and the last note had played, the silence in the hall was deafening. The Sky Toes smiled and smiled and waited for the customary applause. The orchestra members wiped their brows and looked out over the sea of faces and wondered. Then in one movement, it seemed, six thousand people rose to their feet. One pair of hands started to clap, then ten more, then a thousand, and then all twelve thousand hands smacked together.

The Rattoons took their bow. The endless landscape of standing humans was a truly terrifying sight, yet the people seemed to be cheering for them.

35

A GRACEFUL EXIT

They filed off, still waving their right paws in unison. Monk, the last in line, gave a final shuffle and a dig just before he disappeared behind the risers. The audience whooped and shouted with joy.

"We've danced on the biggest stage in the world," said Ella dreamily. "Now I can die happy."

Benny opened his mouth to say something about that time coming soon, but he closed it again. She was right. He too was willing to give up everything else for that one dance.

As the elevator motors began to hum, they slid to the floor and rode down to the basement in total silence, each one reliving the last notes of the horn dying away into silence and the wave after wave of deafening applause.

Woody seemed to be the only one with his wits still about him, so he took over when the elevator ground to a halt. The rest of them were shuffling about in a trance. He held them tight against the riser as the Sky Toes filed off the steps, chattering to one another.

"What happened up there?"

"Were they clapping for us?"

"I heard someone say they saw a bunch of dancing rats."

"You crazy, girl?"

"Each one of you hold on to the other's tail," Woody whispered. "I don't trust you not to go wandering off."

They made it back to the stable by going over the roof of the elevator control room and then wove their way through a group of parked dollies and two costume racks. As they scampered up into the hay, they saw two men yelling at Oliver, who was leaning against the railing of the pen.

"Listen, Bailey, we heard about you. People been saying you're a rat lover from way back, so we figure you brought 'em in. So you're the one who's going to find 'em for me." The man who was talking was chewing on a big dead cigar at the same time, and in between sentences he worked it around from one side of his mouth to the other. Ella and Monk recognized him as Blunt, the man Oliver was always arguing with. The other fellow was skinny and wore a porkpie hat and glasses. He kept poking Oliver in the chest with one of his bony fingers. In the other hand, behind his back, he was holding a big net.

"Keep down," whispered Coleman to the rats. "They're really working him over."

"Now, you tell us where they are right now or we'll hire someone else to manage the rest of these animals."

Coleman put up his head and brayed his disapproval,

which made the two men jump. "Pipe down, big mouth," said Blunt. "So, Bailey, where are you hiding them?"

"I'm not hiding them anywhere," Oliver said coolly. "Those rats have minds and feet of their own, as I expect even you noticed, Blunt. Seems, in fact, the whole audience noticed."

"Well, if I know anything, those rats will come find you, and when they do, you come find us, you hear? You got till the end of this show, and if you don't bring 'em to me by then, you're out. For good." Blunt was chomping so hard on his cigar that little bits of it kept falling out of his mouth.

Monk crawled up next to Ella. "We can't let Oliver lose his job," he whispered in her ear.

She nodded. "Oliver," Ella called. "We're right here. Behind you."

"Keep yourselves hidden, Ella," he squeaked back.

"What did you say?" asked the porkpie hat with another poke.

"Nothing," said Oliver. "Just clearing my throat."

"You weren't making fun of the boss here, was you?" Poke, poke. "You wouldn't want to do that, would you?"

Ella jumped out of the pile of hay, and before Benny could pull her back down, she marched onto the railing.

"Oh, jeez," said Coleman. "Now she's in for it. I can't watch. I hate the sight of blood." He turned away and buried his head in a pile of hay.

"You were asking for me?" she called.

"Ella, I told you to keep down," muttered Oliver.

"There's one of them, boss. The rat with the tap shoes."

The cigar man made a lunge for Ella, but she stepped nimbly out of his way and scampered down to the lower railing.

"No touching," she called. "Just talking. Oliver, tell them we're leaving. We got everything we wanted. One dance on that stage. We'll never bother them again. Promise."

"What's it saying?" asked the porkpie hat.

"SHE is saying you'll never catch her," translated Oliver. "So you might as well start talking. They were great, weren't they? So what's the deal?"

"Oliver, that's not what I said," Ella squeaked.

He motioned her to be quiet. "I have a feeling they don't want you to leave," he told her. "Let's hear them out."

"Where's her buddies?" asked Blunt. "We want to talk to them all at once."

The porkpie hat was sidling closer.

"He's got a net, Ella," Oliver warned.

"I know, I can see it," she said. "He doesn't look too swift on his feet, though."

"What is she saying?" Blunt roared at Oliver.

"She's saying you'd better start talking quick. They'll leave, if that's what you want, but you never know when they might come back. You don't want word to get around that you've got rats in your basement, do you?"

"Bailey, are you an idiot? We don't want rats in the basement. We want these rats up on the big stage. The boss upstairs wants me to sign them to a season contract, and if I don't do it by the next show, he says I'm out on my ear. So stop playing games with me."

Ella's four brothers had joined her on the railing.

"Well, how about that," said Fletcher.

"You mean they don't want to trap us, poison us, set their dogs on us, or hit us with umbrellas?" asked Woody.

"Guess not. You can't blame them," Oliver said with a grin. "You all were fantastic up there, Ella. Never saw anything like it. You should have seen yourselves on that screen. Larger than life."

"Watch out," bleated a sheep. But it was too late. Porkpie jumped out, dropped the net on the lot of them, and pressed the rim into the hay.

"Don't damage them," said Blunt. "They're precious property."

"They aren't anybody's property," yelled Oliver. "If you don't let them go right now, I'll make sure they don't sign any contract. Lift that net. Now."

"Boss?" said Porkpie.

"Just a little insurance, Bailey. Gives us time to talk terms, don't you know?"

The Rattoons lay flat on their backs, staring up through

the netting. "Oliver," squeaked Ella. "If they don't let us out of here right now, we may never be able to dance again. My bottom paw is twisted, and Monk is moaning something terrible."

Oliver relayed the message. "Lift the net," Blunt said. His lips were working the cigar so hard, it looked as if he might swallow it without noticing.

"You sure, boss?" asked Porkpie.

"Stop asking me dumb questions," roared Blunt.

The net came off, and the five rats pulled one another to their feet and dusted off their costumes. Monk did a few stretches, and Fletcher massaged Woody's right shoulder where it had hit the floor.

"We're not coming cheap after that little episode," warned Benny.

o　●　o　●　o

The negotiations lasted fifteen minutes. Oliver was hired on the spot as managing agent, and he insisted on all sorts of provisions that the Rattoons would never have considered. He retained the rights to their movie personalities, got them their own dresser, costume designer, and dressing rooms, and had Ella's name added to the program as special choreographer. Finally, he demanded that the Rattoons' name be listed on the front marquee in four-foot letters.

Porkpie was scribbling notes as fast as he could.

"Rattoons? How do you spell that?" he asked.

"Two *t*'s, two *o*'s," said Oliver.

"And Oliver gets his own office even if our contract is terminated," said Ella.

"I can't tell them that, Ella," said Oliver.

"They want us, they got to put it in."

"Stop squeaking at each other and tell me what you're saying," Blunt said.

He rolled his eyes and clapped his hand to his forehead when he heard that demand. "I need to check with management on this."

"So go check," said Oliver. "I wouldn't suggest you take too long, Mr. Blunt, as the Rattoons are red-hot. Right now they are negotiating with another dance club in the vicinity."

"Oliver!" cried Monk. "That's not true."

"What's that place called? The one you were auditioning for."

"The Boom Boom Room," put in Benny.

"That's the name. Boom Boom Room. Ever heard of it, Blunt? You haven't? I'm surprised. It's one of the hottest new clubs in the city. You don't want to lose them to a place like that. . . ."

"Okay, okay, I agree to all of it," said Blunt. "So they'll start at the next show? The four o'clock."

"Long as you have that contract on my desk for signature before then."

"What desk?" asked Porkpie.

"I think I'll take over that free office down the hall from the music library," said Oliver thoughtfully. "The one with the walnut desk and the four-drawer file. That should suit me fine."

"Go, Oliver," cried Ella.

36

THE RATTOONS

The Rattoons still slept in the Hollow but made their way aboveground through the tail opener every morning and home every night. Occasionally after a really long day, they bedded down in the sheep's pen, but they consistently refused the offer of their own nest in the basement of the Crystal. After a day on the stage, they needed to get back home. A rat could take only so many humans in a day.

"It's the smell of them," Monk explained to Buddy. "You just never can get used to that smell."

The office of Designated Foragers, Fourth Division, issued the Rattoons special transit passes once Buddy appeared at the hearing to explain the situation.

"Go over this for me one more time," said the lieutenant at the hearing. "These Rattoons are a main attraction on a stage aboveground? With humans applauding them?"

"Yes, sir," said Buddy. "Not just any stage either. The Crystal, where six thousand humans stand and cheer them at every show. These five dancing rats could be changing the attitude of humans toward our species."

"I'll believe that when I see it," muttered the lieutenant. "So that's why they couldn't appear at their own hearing?"

"That's right, sir. They do four shows a day up there." He rolled his eyes heavenward. "Their act is projected on screens seventy feet high. Imagine that. Humans applauding for seventy-foot rats."

"It boggles the mind," said the lieutenant. "Something I'd like to see."

"I could arrange that, sir."

"You're not offering me a bribe, young rat, are you?"

"Oh no, sir."

The lieutenant signed the passes and handed them over. "Might take you up on that someday. The missus is crazy about rat tappers."

"You let me know, sir. I'll do what I can."

○　●　○　●　○

The management allowed Oliver to organize a party in the stable for a certain night after the last show. The sheep agreed to lend one of their pens, which was set up for refreshments and dancing.

The Rattoons invited every rat they could think to ask. They sent word to Switchtail, who came down by train in time for the show. He picked up Shadrach on his way through Ratrun Central, and Oliver suggested the two old hoofers watch the whole show from the baggy upper pockets of his jacket so as not to alarm any human members of the audience.

"So you do exist, Mr. Oliver String Bean Bailey," Switchtail said as the orchestra began to file in. "Course I've been telling those kids about you and spreading your name around, but who ever knew if it was all true?"

"I do exist, Mr. Switchtail. And from what the Rattoons have told me, you are also a legend in your own time. The creator of the Rat's Tail himself, sitting right here in my pocket."

"Kids," Switch said with a shrug, but he was clearly pleased. "So my Rattoons have done all right for themselves?"

"You taught them well," said Oliver. "Nicest, hardest-working bunch of kids I've ever had the privilege of managing. And remarkable talent. An entirely different situation from those Acrobrats."

"They draw a crowd down at Ratrun Central," said Shadrach. "All that noise their fans make can disturb a rat's nap."

Just then the lights went down, and the two rats settled into comfortable viewing positions.

Nothing had prepared Switchtail for the sight of his five tappers projected on the huge screens, strutting across the great stage as if they owned the place. Their taps were crisp, their neck snaps clean, and they did what Switch had taught them from the very beginning. Every move they made might as well have been their last because they gave it everything they had, every time. Switch cheered them through "Mistletoe Jazz" and their onstage solo in one of Ella's more complicated jazz combinations for the song "Wood Rat's Christmas Ball."

It had been decided after a special audition with the director that, if an encore were demanded, the Rattoons could take the stage and dance "A Fine Rat Romance." It was a number that consistently brought the audience back to its feet, many of them mopping their tears away with large white handkerchiefs. As the last note of the song faded and Monk's waving paw disappeared around the corner of the curtain, Oliver had to rip a Kleenex in half and hand a piece to the two rats, weeping in his jacket pockets.

"That's their best number," Oliver told Switchtail. "I always know when they're doing it because you can hear the applause down below through all four basement levels."

"It's Art and Sally's music coming right through those children," Switch announced after a long blow of his snout. "Strange that I should feel their spirit moving here. My great-grandfather died when they dug the hole to build this place."

"The Rattoons' dancing honors the history of your noble race," said Oliver. "In the process they may even win over some humans. Look around."

Switch and Shadrach poked their snouts farther out of his pockets to watch six thousand humans stamping their feet and calling the Rattoons' name over and over again.

○   ●   ○   ●   ○

The party started as soon as the Rattoons had shed their costumes and the Crystal had been cleared of humans except for Oliver. Buddy brought the guests through the tail opener and escorted them to the sheep's pen. All evening long, he took small groups upstairs for tours of the Great Chamber and the Palace stage itself, remarking on the weight of the curtain and the number of pipes in the organ.

Lieutenant Vera and the museum squad had been given special leave to attend. Vera told Ella that she would be accepting early retirement next month because she'd found a partner to enter ballroom-dancing competitions.

"He's not Harold, mind you," she said with a sigh. "Nobody can ever replace Harold. But this rat has some nice moves on the floor. And he's younger than I am," she added with a whisper and an elbow in Ella's ribs. "Gives me a whole new lease on life."

After the high emotions brought on by the show, Switchtail and Shadrach retired to a corner of the pen to reminisce over old times. A small flask of some dark liquid was seen passing back and forth between them. Some hours later, they were enticed out to join a tap challenge. Shadrach kept yelling that Switchtail had stolen his steps, but everybody knew, at that time of night, it was just the mash talking.

○   ●   ○   ●   ○

The Acrobrats came swinging in at the last moment, Alfredo tipping his hat left and right and Lalo twirling his whiskers. They greeted Oliver with a certain coolness. Oliver bowed in return but said nothing. He knew from long experience with this crew, the less said the better.

Monk convinced them to stay far away from Lieutenant Vera.

"You were responsible for her mate's death, you know that," he told them sternly. "Your unscheduled show above the steps of the museum."

"I don't know what you're talking about, young rat," said Alfredo, but he looked a little shifty about the eyes.

"We paid our price," growled Arturo. "Just you try hanging by your tail for ten days."

"For a ship rat, we hear that's a vacation in the sun," said Fletcher. "But never mind about that now. This is a party. Have yourself some treats," he said, pointing to the trough. The level of food had already been considerably lowered by the hungry crowd.

"Don't mind if we do," said Alfredo as they slunk off. "Have to keep our energy up. Dangerous work on the wires."

"They haven't changed a bit," said Benny.

210

"Did you expect them to?" asked Fletcher.

"Nope."

○　　●　　○　　●　　○

Through it all the Rattoons remained the same. The attention didn't go to their heads. It went to their feet. They danced themselves into a stupor. Ella had regular consultations with the human choreographer, who helped her develop more modern moves in their repertoire. At first, the Sky Toes staged a ministrike, declaring that they had not been trained by the best teachers in the world to dance with a bunch of rats. But little by little, the Rattoons won them over with their dedication to their art, their tireless rehearsals, their respect for the precision of the line.

Often when the elevator brought them down between numbers, Oliver was waiting below to help with costume changes and to see if they needed water or a quick bite to eat.

"That lady in the fifth row center kept shouting my name," said Fletcher one afternoon. "She was at the show yesterday, too."

"Don't let it go to your head, Fletcher," Benny said. "Remember Napoleon's owner?"

"What about her?"

"She was a lady, too," Woody said wryly.

"Well, maybe humans can change," said Monk. "Look at Oliver."

Oliver gave an elaborate bow.

"Oliver was okay from the start," said Ella. "Thanks to Barney."

"Oliver, do you think humans can change?" asked Benny.

"One by one, I think they can," said Oliver. "If you show them reasons to see things differently."

"What kind of reasons?" asked Monk.

"Five high-stepping musical rats, for example. Now, that's a start. Might be hard to cheer you from fifth row center one day and poison your cousin the next."

They considered that idea in silence for a moment.

"Places, Rattoons," called the stage manager. "Elevator's going up for the sixth number."

In a matter of minutes, the five were standing in a proud line, jazz arms raised, chins lifted, and toes pointed.

Oliver gave them a thumbs-up.

Ella winked.

The elevator motor began to hum, and the Rattoons rose slowly upward.